The Barn Brigade

NORA TISEL FARLEY

DEDICATION

*To the girls of the City of Lakes Waldorf School class of 2011:
Anna, Ava, Elizabeth, Evva, Grace, Gracie, Kristi, Lilly, Mary,
Molly, Pauline, and Zara. You are my best friends, beloved sisters,
and biggest source of inspiration. I love you all, and the memories we
shared together have become a part of this book. I hope you smile
when you read them.*

1

On a dark night in a city called Redfield, in a scummy alley, five girls prepared to rob a store. They pulled up in their dark green van, splattering a brick wall with muddy water. Ella, a wide girl with dark skin and strong arms, jumped out of the driver's door. Twenty seconds later she gave the OK signal, a gentle flick of the wrist, and her four companions piled out. They kept to the shadows as they approached the solemn bricks of the supermarket, careful to stay out of the glaring orange light cast by the ever-watchful streetlamp.

Dawn, their leader, a girl with short brown hair and a cynical expression, led the way to a window on the far wall, a window very familiar to these girls. The broken latch slid open easily and, without a sound, the five burglars hoisted themselves into the employees' lounge. In a uniform fashion the twins Tessa and Sabrina stationed themselves on either side of the window and scanned the room.

Dawn approached the lounge door and put her head down to the crack between door and floor, listening. A curt nod of the head was all the others needed. They filed up behind her and waited as she hesitantly opened the door and looked down the blade of an impossibly long and impossibly sharp carving knife.

Ella swore under her breath and Dawn, too preoccupied by the lethal weapon to tell her off, stayed still long enough for the wielder of the knife to produce a flashlight and train it on her eyes. All was still for all of three seconds; then a foot came out of nowhere and the knife clattered to the ground as its holder clutched at her shin. Rita, the owner of the foot, snickered and snatched the knife from the ground before the strange girl could re-collect herself.

"Don't move." Dawn, finally having gathered her wits, grabbed in the dark for her attacker. Dawn's hand caught something thick, coarse, and hairy. The girl stifled a gasp as her ponytail was yanked and she fell hard on her back. Sabrina grabbed the abandoned flashlight and shone it onto the girl's face, not bothering to avoid dazzling her eyes. The attacker was small, with Asian features overshadowed by a long white scar that slashed her cheek. The girl was maybe eleven years old. Her eyes were squeezed shut against the flashlight's beam. In sympathy, Sabrina finally lowered the light.

"Who are you?" Dawn inquired, placing a hand on both of the girl's shoulders. She went limp and opened one eye, looking into Dawn's intense face and squirming under her stare.

"Get off of me." She had a high voice, or maybe she was just frightened; in any case, Dawn did not oblige.

"What's your name? I'll know if you lie. Are you here alone? Answer!"

The girl opened her other eye turned a defiant gaze on her captor. "I'm alone. No one wants me."

"Don't try to play for sympathy," Ella chided, leaning over Dawn's shoulder. "No one wants any of us, either. Now tell her your name before she gets mad." The girl flushed and stopped squirming, letting herself go limp again on the tiled floor.

"OK, OK, my name's Alyssa, now will you let me up?"

Dawn raised an eyebrow. "Last name?"

"Corsson." Alyssa tried to get up but Dawn was still pressing her to the floor.

"Hey! I told you my real name."

"I know," said Dawn. "But I'm not in the habit of releasing people who stick lethal weapons in my face."

Alyssa sagged. "Sorry."

Rita snickered from Tessa's left and the twins exchanged mirthful glances. Dawn, however, remained composed. "I was going for an explanation."

"I was scared. I thought you might be the police, or the night guard or something."

Dawn snorted and let go of the girl.

"Thanks!" Alyssa pushed herself to her knees and gazed up at the group.

Sabrina looked at her watch. "Speaking of the night guard, she arrives in half an hour. Let's get moving."

Dawn nodded and grabbed Alyssa's arm, hauling her to her feet.

"Hey!"

"I don't trust you; you can be my partner."

"Where's the logic in that? And what are we even doing?"

Sabrina laughed. "What do you think we're doing?"

"How should I know? You just kicked me down."

Sabrina rolled her eyes. "That was actually Rita, not me, and we're here to get food, halfwit." Alyssa blushed again and turned her back on Sabrina who smirked and pulled her sister after her into the canned goods aisle.

Dawn kept hold of Alyssa the whole time they were in the supermarket, carefully pulling food item after food item from the back of the shelf and arranging the front with gloved fingers. Alyssa tried to talk a few times, to pose any one of the multitudes of questions gallivanting around her mind, but each time she was hastily shushed by her tall escort and yanked along once more. Ten hasty minutes of 'shopping' later, Dawn dragged Alyssa to a halt in front of the muffin cabinet, quickly selecting two boxes of double chocolate chip muffins and stuffing them into her already bulging burglar's bag.

The three partnerships converged at the *Employees Only* door and Dawn relinquished custody of Alyssa to Ella so she could check the alleyway.

"What're you going to do with me?" Alyssa whispered as soon as Dawn was out of earshot.

Ella smiled. "You want my guess? I'd say she'll take you with us, but you never can tell with Dawn."

Sabrina's eyes widened in the faint glow of the exit signs and she could barely conceal her disdain when she whispered, "No way are we taking *her* with us. She's like, nine."

"I'm eleven!" Alyssa burst out, and Ella turned away so the younger girl wouldn't see her smirk.

Sabrina snorted. "Same difference. We don't have more room anyway."

"True," Ella said, "but I don't know what else she'd do with her, do you?" Sabrina frowned and shook her head.

"We could just, you know, leave her here."

"Sabrina!" Tessa's shocked reprimand reminded Alyssa of the other twin's presence.

"Nah, she knows too much anyway," Ella said with a casual shrug. Alyssa gave her an incredulous stare.

"I don't know anything," she declared flatly, "and I don't want to come with you."

"Why not?" Ella asked, "Because you've got so much waiting for you at home?" Alyssa looked down.

"See?" Ella said, as if that settled it. "You're coming with us."

Dawn appeared at the doorway, frowning. She drew an insistent finger across her throat to shut them up and the girls obliged. Even Alyssa could see what was expected of her, though she'd never met these girls before. Dawn jerked her head towards the open window and her companions plus Alyssa followed her back the way they'd come. Alyssa was still being held firmly by Ella.

2

The green van was still parked in the delivery driveway of the salon across the street from the grocery store. Alyssa was handed off to Rita so Ella could load the trunk with their plunder. No one spoke just yet and it was clear to the captive Alyssa that speech was not permitted. She was squeezed into the van, sitting on Rita's lap beside Tessa, whose twin Sabrina was seated opposite her. Only once the back door was quietly shut and Ella took her place behind the wheel did the questions start. Finally able to talk, each girl spoke over the others, trying to have her inquiry heard and answered first.

"ENOUGH!" Dawn finally yelled as Ella backed out of the alley and executed a clumsy three-point turn onto the street beyond. "Everyone SHUT UP! I've got this under control." Alyssa took advantage of the momentary silence to ask her primary question.

"Where are you *taking* me?"

Dawn eyed her in the rearview mirror. "Well, first we're going to check alleys, but after that, you're coming home with us. Where else?"

Sabrina lowered her head in order to avoid her sister's *she-did-warn-you-after-all* shrug and Ella's knowing nod in her direction.

"What is alley-checking?" Alyssa asked.

Dawn scrutinized her in the rear view mirror. "We drive through people's alleys and pick up the random junk they're throwing out for trash collection."

"Do you get paid for that?" the newcomer wanted to know. Everyone else laughed. She was beginning to resent being brought along with them.

"No," Ella told her, "we take it home and use it ourselves." She turned the van down a residential alley and all the passengers turned so they could look out the windows. The streetlamps provided a passable glow; Alyssa could see people's trash bins and garages fairly well.

"There!" It was Sabrina, looking out the opposite window at a pile of buckets set out behind someone's garage.

"There are lights on in that house." Dawn was right. The house that belonged to the garage in question was lit up — only a few windows to be sure, but enough to make the thieves a bit wary.

"What do you think?" Dawn asked the van at large. She was answered by a general murmur in the affirmative.

"OK, Rita, you and the new girl are in charge of this one. Go for it."

Rita relinquished her grip around Alyssa's waist but kept a tight hold on one of her arms as she unbuckled her seatbelt and opened the door. She pushed Alyssa off her lap and into the alley in front of her. The night was cold; it seemed colder than it had before they'd robbed the supermarket.

Inside the van, Ella must've pressed a button because the back hatch came up, revealing the groceries, neatly stacked on one side of the trunk, leaving plenty of room for the alley loot. Rita released Alyssa in order to pick up the buckets, leaving her standing in a pool of orange light from the streetlight.

"Oi!" Dawn stuck her head out the window, whisper shouting. "New girl, get out of that light before someone sees you!" Alyssa glanced up at the house. She could see someone in the window, a young man with a curly beard, and he was looking in her direction. She hastily stepped out of sight, hoping with all her might that she hadn't been seen.

Rita handed her the stack of buckets and Alyssa threw them in the back of the van. The door slammed behind her and Rita pulled the seatbelt over them both as Ella stepped on the gas pedal and they pulled out of the alley.

"I swear," Dawn said, "if you ever stand in plain sight like that again I will personally see to it that you are punished severely. You could have been seen!"

Alyssa chose wisely not to tell Dawn about the man in the window who may or may not have been looking at her.

"Sorry."

Tessa yawned. "Hey, Dawn, I'm tired. Can't we just go home now? What else do we need?"

"Well, I was hoping to find some accommodations for our newcomer, but I suppose she can do just fine with what we've got."

"So, you really are taking me home with you? Can't I just go back to living how I was?"

Dawn shook her head. "Nope, no one can know what we've stolen or that we're living together, or especially *where* we're living."

"But I don't know where you're living. Couldn't I just pick up my belongings?"

"That depends." Ella looked at Alyssa in the rear-view mirror, ignoring her first comment. "Do you have anything of value?"

Alyssa thought about it. The few objects she owned were nothing compared to a real place to live, but she disliked being denied, so she said nothing.

"Thought so!" Ella grinned. "Then we'll just bring you with us; no baggage required."

Alyssa frowned. "Why do you want me? You don't even know me. For all you know I could be a serial killer."

"Exactly," said Dawn, curtly, "which is why you're going to tell us your entire life story right now."

Alyssa looked stricken. She bit her lip. "I can't do that," she whispered.

"Sure you can," said Rita, ruffling the younger girl's hair with an awkwardly bent arm. "We've all been through a lot and nothing you can say will shock us." Tessa gave Rita a dirty look and reached for Alyssa's hand, holding it in both of hers. She looked into Alyssa's small, round face, her eyes lingering on the impressive scar.

"We can go first, if you want. Sabrina and I don't mind telling our story now, right?" She glanced at her sister for confirmation; Sabrina didn't look at her but Tessa went ahead anyway.

Alyssa shrugged. "Whatever — just get it over with."

"OK." Tessa smiled sadly. "To start with, my name's Teresa. Please call me Tess, or Tessa. That's my twin sister Sabrina; she's eleven minutes older than me. We're fourteen. Up until a year and a half ago we lived with our parents."

Here Sabrina gave a derisive snort and turned to face the window.

"Well, there's no use denying it," Tessa told her. "It's the truth." Sabrina made a small shrugging motion that translated roughly to "Fine, just get on with the story," so Tessa did.

"None of us really got on too well, except for Sabrina and me. We used to hide in the basement together when they threw things." She said it in such a nonchalant way, it was obvious she'd told her story many times, or maybe she was just used to the idea.

"Our mom used to get totally drunk and yell at us and smash stuff and our dad kind of had, well, *problems* let's say, and he'd just kind of fight her for the sake of fighting her."

"That's... terrible," Alyssa cut in. "Why didn't they just get a divorce?"

"They did, eventually, but it wasn't a clean one and they chose to share custody of us. We didn't want to live with either of them so we staged a temper tantrum at each house in turn, saying we were going to go live with the other parent."

"And they didn't notice you weren't there?" Alyssa cocked her head.

"They wouldn't talk to each other. I doubt they've found out yet, and even if they have I don't think they'd do anything about it. Well, Mom might, but that's only if she's stopped drinking and I can't see that happening."

Here Tessa stopped and glanced at her sister, who was still looking out the window. "You want to tell the rest?"

Sabrina didn't even turn around, she just shook her head and it occurred to Alyssa that there might be tears in her eyes, making her throat go tight — but then again, maybe not; Tessa seemed so calm about it.

"OK then," Tessa said, returning to her story. "We pretty much lived on the streets here in Redfield until ten months ago, when Sabrina tried to pickpocket Rita here," Tessa jerked a thumb at the girl next to her, "and we got caught up with *this* crowd." Tessa looked expectantly at Alyssa, still gripping the younger girl's small, coffee-colored hand in hers.

"Are you ready now?" she asked. Slowly, with a sigh, Alyssa nodded.

"On one condition," she said, sounding much more confident that anyone expected. "The rest of you have to tell me your stories too."

There was an edgy silence in the van that lasted for almost five seconds before Rita shrugged as well as she could with Alyssa on her lap and said, "I'm game."

Ella agreed, avoiding Dawn's eye as she navigated a set of railroad tracks. No one looked at the leader, who kept her head down as she gave her consent.

"I'll start, I guess." Rita took a deep breath and squeezed Alyssa around the middle, momentarily cutting off her supply of air.

"I'm Rita Avis. I'm fifteen years old. I was in an orphanage when I was little. I don't know who my biological parents were. I was a foundling."

"Basically," Sabrina broke in sarcastically, "no one wanted her so she was dumped at a hospital for someone who did."

Tessa sent an indignant elbow into her sister's ribs.

Unexpectedly, Rita agreed with Sabrina. "Yeah, I was... But anyway, that doesn't matter because I was accepted for foster care when I was five. I went to live with two women originally from Uganda named Masami and Namono." Here, Rita leaned her forehead on the back of Alyssa's head, biting her lip; it took her a minute to continue. "They are a lesbian couple. Do you know what that means?"

Alyssa nodded, careful not to bump Rita's nose.

"Well, in Uganda, being gay or lesbian is worse than setting a house on fire or robbing a bank or even killing someone."

"What Rita is trying to say," Sabrina interrupted once again, "is that, in Uganda they enact the *death penalty* for loving someone of the same gender. It's so stupid."

"It's more than stupid," Ella said fervently from behind the wheel. "It's despicable."

Rita took a deep breath and Dawn shifted uneasily in her seat. Apparently it was unlike Rita to get upset in any degree. "They emigrated to America so they wouldn't be killed." Rita swallowed painfully. "I lived with Masami and Namono for eight years. They were like my real parents; I learned everything from them. But, right after I turned fourteen, Namono's visa was revoked and she had to return to Uganda or risk being chased by the law." Rita closed her eyes and hugged Alyssa even tighter, as if she were a teddy bear.

"Masami went with her, and since they hadn't adopted me, I was sent back to stay in the Social Services Center orphanage until they could return, *if* they could return. They were totally honest with me. Namono told me she didn't know if they'd ever be able to come back." A tear slipped between Rita's dark blonde eyelashes, slipping down her cheek as she continued in a defeated voice.

"I haven't seen or heard from either of them since. I don't know what happened to them. For all I know my moms could be dead."

"I told you not to say that kind of thing." Tessa put an arm around her friend. "It'll only get you depressed, and you know it's probably not true."

Rita was crying in earnest now, clutching Alyssa like a life ring and being hugged by the protective arm of Tessa.

"I'm OK, I'm OK." Rita gulped for air and Alyssa hoped she wasn't drooling in her hair. "Well, anyway, after a few months at the orphanage I couldn't take it anymore and ran away." Rita wiped her eyes. "I got lucky. When I tried to hitchhike out of town, Ella was the one who picked me up." Rita gave the driver a quivery smile. "And I guess that's it. I'm sorry I got so worked up."

"You have every right to get worked up!" Tessa patted her shoulder and Rita raised her head. "You're next, Alyssa."

"I don't know if I can compete with that story." Alyssa rubbed her chin.

"It's not about competing," Dawn said firmly. "It's about the truth. Tell us what happened." For some reason that made Ella laugh, a surprisingly bitter sound. She cleared her throat.

"I'm sorry, Alyssa, please begin."

"OK, I guess." Alyssa seemed to be gathering herself. "I lived in a totally normal family until last year. One day my mother and I went to an art museum. It was supposed to be a special outing, just the two of us, because my dad was on a trip. I remember we saw a painting by Picasso that looked like a sheep with a moustache."

"She's dodging the point," Sabrina pointed out, rudely. Tessa elbowed her again.

"I'm going, already!" Alyssa complained. "We went down in an elevator. There was no one else inside. It didn't sound right; there was a strange scraping noise coming from the shaft. Then it dropped; I don't remember much else." Alyssa subconsciously stroked the scar that disfigured the right half of her face; she spoke with an unnaturally flat voice, as if all the retellings of this adventure had watered down its gravity. "They took me to the emergency room, but for my mom it was already too late. I was still in the hospital when they held her funeral."

"That's so awful!" Tessa squeezed Alyssa's hand again. Alyssa shrugged, obviously uncomfortable.

"That's where this scar came from, anyway. There was a lot of nerve damage to my face." Five pairs of eyebrows shot up as their eyes widened in alarm and pity. Alyssa kept her face towards the softly vibrating floor as she went on. "When I was discharged from the hospital, my father was different than he was before. I don't know what happened to him." Here her voice broke. She'd told of her injury a hundred times but this was new territory, new pain.

"He drank a lot, and locked himself in his office or the basement for days at a time. I thought he was dead too sometimes but then he started to hit me and scream at me and break things, and I started wishing… he *was* dead." Alyssa brought her knees up to her chest and hugged them, resting her chin on the denim hills. Tessa's eyes brimmed as she rubbed her smooth thumbs over the backs of Alyssa's little fists. No one denied what Alyssa had said. No one tried to tell her it wasn't true, or wasn't serious, or wasn't possible; it was a mark of how grave their own experiences had been that they didn't have to question such a horrid history.

"That's mostly it. I ran away and lived in a public park. I was about to steal food when you guys came up behind me."

"That reminds me," Dawn said, twisting round to look at Alyssa, whose face was now obscured by her knees, "how did you get into that supermarket? We use the window, obviously, but I've been looking for a less risky entry point for a while."

Alyssa sighed, not lifting her head. "There's a skylight above the warehouse; it's cracked open for ventilation. I just forced it open further and climbed through."

"What about the screen?" Ella asked, looking both ways as they came to an intersection on the way out of town.

"I took it off. It should still be like that."

Dawn whirled around. "You *what*?" Her tone was lethal.

"I took it off." Alyssa squeezed her knees even tighter, puzzled by the older girl's rage.

"And you *left* it like that?"

"You guys had me captive!"

"You could have said *something*. We should go back and fix it."

Ella groaned. "No, Dawn, it's fine, they won't even notice and I don't want to drive all the way back there. Besides, the night guard will be there by now." Dawn frowned, the harsh light of a street lamp illuminating her worried expression.

"OK, I guess, but if we get busted…" She didn't bother to finish; even Alyssa knew what would happen if they were caught. They were silent, reflecting on this possibility.

"Don't stress out about it — they probably won't even notice. Anyway, I guess I'm next to join the Pity Party." Ella grinned. "My story's not nearly as grim as yours. I don't know if I've told you my name yet. I'm Ella Rowett."

"Nice to meet you," Alyssa replied, only because there seemed nothing else to say.

Ella snickered, "I'm supposed to be in college this year. I was last year." Here she seemed to lose her train of thought for a minute before shaking her head and continuing.

"My dad raised me and my big brother. I never knew my mom but apparently she took all the money we had when she left, so we were kind of poor. Somehow I never questioned how my school funds were being paid, until my dad got thrown in prison for check forgery."

Alyssa's eyes widened. "Wait, so he paid for your education with stolen money?"

"Essentially," Ella explained. "He pretended to be someone he wasn't so that he could use their bank account to pay my fees. Kind of stupid of him, really.

"I thought the authorities might decide I'd been in on his plot and arrest me, too. I'm nineteen, so they could have, but they would've traced me if I'd gone to live with my brother and I didn't have any money for rent. So I took this van before the bank could, put on dealer plates instead of the real ones and painted it green. I lived out of this van for about a month before picking up Rita as a hitchhiker. She stuck around and before you know it, we'd run into Dawn and it just sort of snowballed. We moved in with her and we're still there."

Ella fell silent, staring determinedly at the road ahead.

"Well," Alyssa finally asked, "where *do* you guys live, anyways?"

"In a barn," Rita said cheerfully. She seemed to have let all remnants of the recent conversation leave her mind, at least for the time being. Alyssa twisted to look back at the carefree girl sitting beneath her.

"I'm not falling for that, you know. Just because I'm younger than you doesn't mean I'm stupid."

"She's not lying," Sabrina said. "You'll see soon; we're almost there."

Alyssa shrugged noncommittally and turned her slightly puffy eyes to Dawn. "Your turn. How'd you end up this way?"

There was a tense moment in which everyone seemed to stiffen, waiting for something they weren't sure would come, and then...

"No."

Dawn said it with a quiet conviction that made her refusal obvious, but Alyssa wasn't satisfied.

"Hey, you promised!" Alyssa was outraged and indignant. Dawn looked at her in the rear view mirror.

"Didn't you ever read *The Lord of the Rings*?" she asked. Puzzled, Alyssa shook her head.

"Pity," Dawn said, "but just because I promised, doesn't mean I told the truth. I'm not telling you anything."

"But that's not fair!" Alyssa clenched her fists again. "We all told you our stories!"

"I already knew all but yours, and there's no way you're going to get me to feel guilty. I'll tell you my last name, it's Allerman, but that's all you're going to get."

A subtle look from Tessa told Alyssa that Dawn was, right. Not *in* the right by any means, but she knew her own terms and she stood by them through all conditions. Alyssa groaned, acknowledging her defeat.

3

The girls fell into a murky silence for the rest of the drive. It wasn't long — about five minutes. Ella turned the van off the road and drove behind a convenient copse of evergreens. Alyssa, raising her head from her knees, saw that her captors had indeed been telling the truth. A huge red barn loomed above her, all peeling paint and rotting beams.

Before she could say anything, Rita dumped her unceremoniously onto Tessa's lap and vacated the vehicle. Alyssa watched as Rita's blonde ponytail bobbed in the darkness up to the barn door. She couldn't see very well, but in a moment a single bare light bulb went on inside and Rita could be seen holding open one of the heavy double doors.

Ella put the van in reverse and backed into the barn, skillfully avoiding the large piles of flotsam and jetsam concealed within. Rita closed the doors again and used a pulley to lower a large board into two brackets on the inside: a barricade. Seeing Alyssa's nervous glance, Tessa laughed kindly.

"That's not to keep you in, if that's what you're worried about," she said. "It's to keep anyone else out."

That did almost nothing to relieve Alyssa's qualms, but she followed the others out of the van nonetheless.

"How'd you get the power in here?" she asked, looking around at the emergency light bulb that glowed above the trash can in the corner, and the cluster of cords leading down through a trap door in the floor.

"Ella," Dawn said simply. "She's a master with anything electrical or mechanical like that. We're pirating off the power lines by the road. Before she and Rita came, I used candles and flashlights." She smirked, an interesting contortion of her pretty face. She turned and opened the trap door Alyssa had noticed earlier. The first light clicked off as what appeared to be a basement light turned on and the girls filed down a ladder to the room below.

"Welcome!"

Rita held out a mocking hand to the cinderblock room below the barn. Five cots lined the far wall, all neatly covered in sleeping bags of different colors. To the immediate left was a large and rickety bookcase, completely overflowing with literature of every sort. On one side of the room a miniature chemistry table held a portable stove and a large carboy full of water. On the other, a whiteboard easel covered with what looked like an intricate map stood before a low table under which lay five cushions. The corner to the right of the ladder was covered in a curtain made up of six sewn-together beach towels.

Alyssa stared, bemused, as the other girls dispersed throughout the room. Sabrina and Rita converged on a shelf beside the curtain, grabbing tooth and hairbrushes and proceeding to brush their teeth in the tiny sink of the chemistry table. Tessa, who had carried half the groceries down the ladder, went to the other side of the chemistry table and began unloading. Ella went with her toting the rest of the food. Dawn disappeared behind the curtain. It was as if Alyssa had suddenly vaporized and these strange thieves had gone back to their normal lives — as normal as this kind of life could get.

Alyssa sat down, leaning against the wall, and gave a long, heavy sigh. She hadn't had many things in the park where she lived, but what there was she would have wanted to bring with her: the old down sleeping bag, the storm radio which doubled as a flashlight, her roasting fork. She sighed again and brought her knees up to her chest once more, folding her arms around them and waiting, for the thousandth time, to be noticed.

4

Roy Corsson was not a man who did much of anything, at least not anymore. His wife was dead and his daughter had vanished without a trace. He had nothing left but his empty house and his full bottle.

It was eight o'clock, but either way, Roy didn't care, at least until the phone rang.

"H'lo?" His greeting was slurred. He hardly noticed.

"Mr. Corsson?" The voice was sharp, probably female, though in his state it was hard to tell.

"Yeah, s'me, whaddaya want?"

"I'm calling to inquire about the whereabouts of your daughter Alyssa. She hasn't been at school for several weeks. We assumed it was a relapse of her injury, but I thought I'd call, just to make sure."

It was the school secretary. Roy swore.

"Excuse me?" The woman was way too perky for this hour — oh, never mind, it was only eight o'clock.

"Yur wasting yur time, I dunno where she is either. She ran off 'bout a month ago."

"Are you sure, Mr. Corsson? Because if that's true I have no choice but to report her — and you — to Social Services."

"Y'do that, ma'am, I'm looking forward to see'n her again."

"Given the circumstances, Mr. Corsson, I very much doubt that your daughter will be given back into your custody. Good evening, sir. I'm sure the proper authorities will be in touch."

"G'bye."

The phone clicked as he hung up. The woman on the other end tapped a pencil as she thought. In his condition, Roy Corsson was hardly reliable but it would still be a good idea to check, just to be sure. She looked up the number for Redfield Social Services and dialed.

5

The alarm clock rang at seven o'clock the next morning and Dawn sat bolt upright, groping for the cord with the light switch beside her cot. Alyssa, opening one eye from her makeshift pallet on the floor, wondered if Dawn had had a nightmare. It became apparent that this was not the case as the older girl briskly swung her legs out of bed and cracked her neck to either side, rolling her shoulders and preparing herself for her next task which, as it turned out, was to rouse her companions.

Dawn had a unique philosophy: every person was best awoken in a different way. She had in fact found, through trial and error, the correct way to wake each of her fellow Barn dwellers. Alyssa watched as she moved systematically down the row.

Ella was first. Her sleeping bag was unzipped and unceremoniously torn away. Then came Rita who got a drop of cold water in her upturned ear. Sabrina, the next in line, was subjected to a light slap across the face and Tessa to a vigorous shaking. Dawn turned to see Alyssa watching her.

"Ah," was all she said.

Once everyone was awake, Dawn disappeared behind the curtain, telling Alyssa to wait. Just as they had done the night before, the girls took turns in what seemed to be routine, beginning with Sabrina and Ella scampering up the ladder to use the outhouse while Rita and Tessa washed their hands with the carboy and began to prepare breakfast.

Alyssa stood beside the curtain while Dawn changed out of her black clothes from the night before. Last night Tessa had assured Alyssa that the whole work group thing would get sorted out today. Alyssa didn't really care; she wasn't sure if she liked these girls. Their manner was too… military, almost like they were at a boot camp instead of a worn out old barn. A hand landed hard on Alyssa's shoulder and she jumped. Dawn, the owner of the hand, just smirked.

"OK, as you may have observed, this curtain here is our changing room." She swept her hand wide and ushered Alyssa back into the corner where two baskets dominated the hard dirt floor.

"This one," Dawn said, indicating the basket on the right, "is for dirty clothes, anything you take off goes in there. This one," she pointed to the other basket, "is all clean clothes; just wear whatever fits." Dawn left her behind the curtain and went to scrutinize the cooking of breakfast.

"What are you making?" Dawn looked into the frying pan that sat neatly atop the glowing coil of the portable stove.

"I'm not sure what it is," Rita told her cheerfully "but I'm following the directions." She held up a cylindrical, sausage-like package about half full of a firm yellow substance.

"That's called polenta, Rita. It's made of cornmeal. You should put some tomato sauce on it."

"OK!" Rita got down on her knees and rummaged around below the tiny sink. Dawn rolled her eyes at Tessa who shrugged good-naturedly and began flipping the polenta rings. " Didn't know either."

Alyssa emerged from the curtain wearing a pair of mint green running shorts with a belt and a Redfield University sweatshirt.

Dawn curled her lip. "You look ridiculous."

"You don't have to rub it in," Alyssa grumbled, crossing her arms.

Ella turned away to hide her grin— because Dawn was right, the red and purple sweatshirt clashed terribly with the perky shorts.

Sabrina's foot appeared on top on the ladder and Ella followed her as soon as she was low enough.

"What's for breakfast?" Ella asked

"Polenta," Sabrina diagnosed with disdain.

"How on earth do you know that?" Her sister turned to her with a puzzled expression; Sabrina gave her a cynical look. "We're the supposed Italians around here."

Tessa took the small can of tomato sauce Rita handed her, and stared at Sabrina in mock defense. "We're only *half* Italian, and I'm not exactly a culinary genius." Tess giggled as her sister shook her head in defeat.

Dawn snorted. "I'll let you two work that one out." She pulled Alyssa towards the ladder.

While the light in the basement was provided by a cluster of emergency bulbs encased in yellow plastic grating and supported by mass amounts of duct tape, the light in the upper Barn was thin, filtering through gaps in the boards, illuminating the dust particles that hung in the early morning air. It gave the impression that time was standing still. Alyssa's legs sprouted goose bumps in the sudden cold and she wished she'd been able to find a pair of pants that fit.

The barricade had been lifted from the door and now hung on its pulley just above the doorframe. The doors were shut and Dawn opened a tiny peephole to look around before beckoning Alyssa to follow her outside. They walked around the side of the Barn where there stood a tiny structure made of plywood. A purple curtain fluttered over one wall, standing in for a door.

"This is the outhouse," Dawn explained. "I won't go into details, but basically every few months we dig a new hole and move this building over it, filling up the old hole. It's not fancy, or even *nice*, but it works. Go on."

Alyssa slipped behind the curtain. The building had a floor, but half of it was elevated like in a porta-potty, only here there was no seat — just a hole in the board. Alyssa grimaced.

After she emerged Dawn brought her to a pump about ten feet away and worked the handle up and down while Alyssa washed her hands underneath the spray.

"Aren't you going to go?" Alyssa looked up at Dawn. She could see the older girl's muscles as she pulled on the handle. They were toned, and not a little intimidating.

"Yes."

"Then why didn't you?" Dawn frowned as if she thought it a stupid question.

"Why do you think we go in pairs? It's so that we can keep this handle clean. You'll pump for me next."

In her mind, Alyssa froze; she wasn't sure if she was strong enough to work the pump and wasn't looking forward to finding out. She dried her hands on her overlarge sweatshirt while Dawn used the outhouse, then, when the older girl came out she bravely reached up for the handle — near the very end for maximum leverage — and yanked it down with all her might. To her surprise, it moved and she heard water splash onto the ground where Dawn was leaning. The arm moved back up of its own accord and Alyssa had to jump to bring it back down again. By the time Dawn's hands were clean, Alyssa was grateful for her small green running shorts and wishing she could take off the sweltering University sweatshirt.

Back in the Barn Rita and Tessa were already dressed and Sabrina was flipping the polenta for the last time. Ella moved the table from in front of the whiteboard to the middle of the room and set it with six plastic plates, cups and forks. Dawn took over the steaming polenta as Sabrina dove for the curtain and Ella positioned the cushions around the low table as seats. The final group left for the outhouse and

Alyssa watched in fascination as Dawn tossed the little discs of corn around in bubbling tomato sauce.

"Don't just stand there," Dawn said, noticing her. "Fill the cups with water; you see the carboy?" Alyssa did, so she grabbed two cups and brought them to the sink.

By the time Tessa and Ella returned from the outhouse the frying pan was sitting on the table and Rita was practically drooling from hunger.

"This is *good*!" Tessa remarked with mild surprise as she bit into one of the yellow rings on her plate. Sabrina smirked, "I told you so."

"Um, would any of you want to explain to me what you do here?" Alyssa asked timidly. She was the only one without a cushion and the others looked down on her with varied expressions of confusion, annoyance and pity.

"Don't look at me like that. I'm new here. You guys just dragged me out here without even asking me. So what do I do now that I'm here?"

Dawn's lip moved in a half smile. "We don't *do* anything. We're not some kind of organization or something like that. We're just here because we have nowhere else to go. We're trying to survive."

Alyssa was silent for a moment, collecting her thoughts. "I guess you just seem really, I dunno, military, like you're training for something." Everyone but Dawn laughed, an unexpected reaction. Backs were patted and eyes were wiped. Alyssa waited for them to quiet down.

"You're right!" Ella choked out, "It's totally like that." Rita nodded and Sabrina pounded her fist on the table. Tessa snickered apologetically. Alyssa turned to Dawn who was staring defiantly at the table, and cocked her head inquiringly.

Dawn looked up. "Be quiet!" The Barn echoed with the final strains of their laughter as the girls straightened their backs and attempted to compose themselves.

"There you go again! You're so... uniform." Alyssa looked at her companions in confusion, and then turned an accusatory gaze on Dawn. "Are you responsible for this?"

Dawn looked pleased with herself, if a little defensive. "Why do you think this Barn is so clean? Why do you think we all feel safe here? Why do you think we're still *alive*? It's how we live. I know you didn't volunteer for it but I'm telling you for your own good: you better go along with it."

"Perhaps you could tell me the rules." Alyssa tried to be as polite as possible. Dawn seemed scarier every minute Alyssa spent with her.

"I'll let the others do that — they *ought* to know by now." With that, the leader set into her polenta with unnecessary vigor.

6

"As you saw, we all wake up at seven every day." Ella reached for another dirty plate and dunked it into the wash water. "Then," she continued, "we take it in shifts to cook, dress and use the outhouse. After breakfast, as you see, one team washes dishes, and the other," she gestured with a soapy hand, "makes the beds and cleans the Barn."

"I think I've got it. So I'm partners with Dawn before breakfast and you and Tessa after breakfast?"

Tessa leaned over from her place at the drying rack. "That's right."

"And after this? What do we do next?"

"Well, we usually do exercises in the gym for about an hour, then come back here for tutorial. Then we have lunch."

Alyssa frowned. "Why do you exercises? And what's tutorial?"

"We exercise because Dawn makes us," Ella explained, "and tutorial is a lot like school."

Alyssa wrinkled her nose.

"But usually a lot more fun," Tessa added hastily.

"I just hope you're right," the youngest girl muttered as she passed Ella another plate. "So, what comes after that?"

"Free time."

Alyssa hadn't expected that. "What's the catch?" she asked shrewdly. Tessa glanced at Ella and the two of them grinned conspiratorially.

"OK, now I'm really scared. What is it?"

"Well," Tessa began, wiping off two forks at a time and stowing them in a mug behind the carboy, "you know how Dawn grabbed your ponytail last night?"

Alyssa winced, but nodded.

"I think she might try and give you a haircut."

"No way, she can't do that!" Alyssa reached protectively for the thick, slightly tangled bunch of hair that coiled inside her sweatshirt's hood. "I won't let her."

Ella snickered to herself, "That's what Sabrina said, too."

Alyssa looked over her shoulder at Tessa's twin who was busy erasing the whiteboard. Sabrina's dark brown hair was tied neatly in two bunches just touching her shoulders.

"*Dawn* did that?" Alyssa was impressed. "How'd she learn so well?"

Tessa shrugged. "She's good at everything — you saw her cooking breakfast."

"Where is she, anyway?" Alyssa asked, dunking the last cup into the tomato-y wash water.

"Probably upstairs setting up the gym for our workout."

"The gym is… upstairs? I thought you meant we were going to the one in Redfield."

"Nope," Ella laughed. "We try to stay here as much as possible 'cause it's risky to be spotted. We take a trip into town about once every two weeks."

Ella let the dishwater out of the sink and waited for it to drain away before bending down to open the cupboard below. Tessa grabbed the nearly empty carboy and started towards the ladder.

"What're you doing?" Alyssa squatted down beside the dark-skinned girl just as Ella stood up, hauling with her a large, bottlenecked vessel full of the dishwater they'd just used.

"We don't have a drain so we have to empty the waste water from this thing every day. It gets pretty nasty, especially because we all brush our teeth in here."

"Eew! You didn't have to tell me that!"

"Why not? Wouldn't you rather know?" Ella had a point, but Alyssa refused to acknowledge it, climbing the ladder ahead of her so she wouldn't be obliged to help lift the scummy tank. Her efforts were wasted, for as soon as she got to the top Ella instructed her to grab onto it from above and get it up that way. It wasn't wet or anything but Alyssa still felt gross after touching it and washed her hands several times at the pump once Tessa had finished filling up the carboy.

"Can you help me with this?" Tessa indicated the carboy as Alyssa followed her back into the Barn. "Here, I'll go down first. You just lower it down to me." Alyssa knelt down on the cold cinderblocks as Tessa slid down the ladder.

"OK, I'm ready. Send it down."

Alyssa gritted her teeth, grabbed the bulky container by the short stem, and succeeded in pushing it over the trapdoor's hole. It was a LOT heavier than she'd anticipated and she struggled not to drop it as her arms were yanked practically out of their sockets.

"Some help, please?" In a strained voice, Alyssa managed to appeal to Ella in the barn behind her.

Ella snorted but put down the empty waste tank and placed her hands over Alyssa's, lowering the carboy down until Tessa could brace her hands around it. She was strong and took it with little effort. Alyssa marveled as she started down the ladder after Tessa.

The exercises that Ella had described were not long in coming. As soon as Rita finished straightening the row of shoes that lived beside the ladder, Dawn's head appeared at the trapdoor, upside-down with her short hair forming a comical helmet around her evil grin.

"Workout time!" She sounded *way* too happy about it, but nonetheless the girls obediently followed her up the two ladders to the gym in what must have once been a hayloft. It certainly no longer contained hay; it didn't even look like a gym. The floor was covered almost completely with mismatched rugs, obviously compiled from the unsuspecting citizens who put them out for solid waste collection. In the far corner hung a climbing rope and across from it was an orderly pile of disorderly exercise supplies. Among them: a resistance strap, a couple of rusty hand weights and a heavily duct-taped yoga ball.

"Line up." The command went unneeded for most, but Alyssa hastily found a place on the end closest to the trap door beside Sabrina. The older girl turned an unnecessary glare at her, but Alyssa had no time to worry about it.

Dawn stood facing of them, her wicked smile still in place.

"Just so you know, Alyssa, we start with stretching, then aerobics for stamina and finally strength training. Just follow what I do."

That proved easier said than done. During the stretching it was simple enough just to do her best to follow Dawn's example — no matter that she couldn't actually get into most of the positions that the others managed with a nonchalance that wasn't lost on the newcomer. The first aerobic section proved to be a kickboxing routine Dawn had picked up somewhere. Alyssa's elbows popped out every time she punched and she had trouble following the intricate choreography with only Dawn's breathless counting to keep time. Next Rita switched places with the leader and proceeded to guide the barn-dwellers through a crazy hopping dance, which Alyssa suspected was made up on the spot.

By the time strength training came around, Alyssa had removed her sweatshirt to reveal the baggy gray tank top she'd donned beneath it. She was breathing hard and her skin felt clammy as Dawn reassumed the lead and instructed them to lie on the ground. She called out commands for different kinds of sit-ups that Alyssa'd never even heard of. It was the most she could do just to keep up with the basic crunches they did after that. The last thing Dawn had them do was push-ups: fifty of them. Alyssa tried her best, but barely managed five, earning herself a scornful look from Dawn, a derisive snort from Sabrina, and a bit of advice from Tessa.

"Try putting your hands out farther. You're straining you elbows; yeah, like that." After five minutes of subtle coaching Alyssa was able to complete fifteen push-ups before her arms gave out and Tessa permitted her to join the others in the basement for the mysterious tutorial.

Still breathing hard, Alyssa plopped down on a cushion and made herself focus on Ella, who stood before them with marker in hand. Ella spent the next half hour drawing a diagram of a car's battery on the whiteboard and explaining exactly how to disassemble it. It was the most useful lesson Alyssa had ever experienced.

"Class dismissed!" Ella finally pronounced with an ironic flourish of her hand.

Lunch was prepared in the same manner as breakfast, in two shifts, this time with the twins and Dawn setting the table while the rest of them prepared a single can of asparagus soup.

"Are you sure that's going to be enough?" Alyssa asked, looking into the pan where bubbled the light green concoction. She had never cared for asparagus.

"We're on a ration," Ella told her.

"You're kidding!" Alyssa was incredulous. "Why on earth are you doing that?"

"I thought I told you. We only go into Redfield twice a month. We've got to make the most of what we've got."

"Look on the bright side." Rita leaned around Ella's back to talk to Alyssa. "You can always have as much water as you want!"

"Oh, brilliant." Alyssa's sarcasm was not disguised.

The soup turned out to be tastier than Alyssa had expected and there was relative silence punctuated with soup slurping while the girls ate.

"So, what do we do next?" Alyssa finally asked, putting down her spoon.

"I have a plan," said Dawn, unhelpfully.

"What kind of plan?" Alyssa sensed she was pushing it, that Dawn was scarier than she looked, but she didn't want to have to tolerate this lack of detail.

"Never you mind. I'll tell you later." Dawn's tone was sharp, and she avoided meeting anyone's eyes.

"Yes sir, Lieutenant Colonel!" Alyssa meant it to be a sarcastic comment, but suddenly realized it was closer to the truth than she'd first imagined. "Do any of you know what a Lieutenant Colonel is the head of?" Alyssa turned to her companions and cocked her head, sending her long black ponytail dangerously close to Rita's soup.

"Uh… a battalion, I think. Or maybe a brigade. Does that sound right?" Ella chewed her lip.

"I think so," said Rita, gathering the empty bowls and standing up to take them to the sink. "I might be wrong though."

"In that case," Alyssa announced, "you guys need a name."

"Oh, good grief." Sabrina put a hand over her eyes.

"You're a Barn Battalion, no, a Barn Brigade." Alyssa was satisfied with her pronouncement. She grinned and nodded decisively.

"No," Tessa said, putting her arm playfully around Alyssa's shoulders, "you're one of 'us' now. *We're* a Barn Brigade."

Sabrina frowned disgustedly. "You do know how cliché that sounds, right?"

They all laughed, except for Dawn. She was already at the sink, her strong hands deep in icy wash water, her back resolutely turned.

The washing up went quickly and after all the dishes were clean and the table was back in place against the west wall Dawn clapped her hands, seemingly recovered from her pout. "Rita!"

The blonde girl looked up, curious. "Yeah? What do you want?"

"Get out the sewing kit. Tess, go up and get that bag of fabric, and bring it down here."

"Alright then." Tessa seemed to have entirely recovered from the rigors of the previous hour and she scampered up the ladder happily to retrieve the fabric.

Dawn's hand landed on Alyssa's shoulder and she jumped, remembering what Ella had said during breakfast clean-up. Her hand jumped instinctively to her ponytail.

Dawn looked mildly surprised, "Don't panic; I'm good at it."

"How'd you know I knew what you're going to do?" Alyssa squeaked.

"Your expression," Dawn laughed. "Who told you?"

"Ella," Alyssa admitted, and Dawn rolled her eyes and turned to accept a large garbage bag from Tessa.

"Take out the big sheet and spread it on the ground. Rita, I want you to find anything in that bag big enough for a bed." Both girls did as they were told and Alyssa say down in the middle of the sheet as Dawn instructed.

"Why do you need to cut it?" Alyssa asked as the leader began to brush out her hair.

"Because it's too long. You could practically stuff a pillow with it. Someone could use it against you. I also don't see you protesting."

Alyssa realized Dawn was right. Something about Dawn made it clear that you didn't want to disagree with her, that she always made the right decisions. Maybe it was the way she only ever smiled at someone else's expense or the way all the other girls, even Ella, who was two years her senior, did everything she said.

Dawn called for a different brush, then a comb, then a bowl of water and finally, for a pair of scissors. Alyssa held her breath and closed her eyes; she hadn't had a serious haircut since she was six. The first thing Dawn did was to hold her hair in a bunch and attack it just below Alyssa's shoulders, severing a majority of the hair in one go. Alyssa winced, but didn't open her eyes.

Dawn's scissors didn't make the crisp sound the salon ones did but it seemed she was doing a good job, for as soon as Alyssa dared to open her eyes, she saw not only a ring of silent spectators and an abundance of black hair scattered over the sheet, but the older girl's careful fingers, gently making the final adjustments to her handiwork.

"There." She said at last, and ushered Alyssa behind the curtain. Everyone crowded in behind them and Alyssa saw Rita crane her neck to see the reaction brought on by the haircut.

It was pretty good! Alyssa had to admit that Dawn knew what she was doing. Her hair was maybe a foot and a half shorter, coming to hang wetly around her chin. There were layers on the sides and her part had been moved an inch to the left. She looked older, less presumptuous, like she actually knew what she was talking about.

"Thanks."

Dawn looked smug and gratified. "You're welcome."

7

"Rita, I told you to find some fabric. Where is it?" Dawn looked up with furrowed brows. Rita hastened to show her the mass of brown calico she'd unearthed.

"What should I do with it?" Rita wanted to know.

Dawn scrutinized the fabric, measuring and snipping in her mind until she found the perfect shape.

"Put it on the ground and cut it into as big an oval as you can. Alyssa, help me with this hair."

It was the first time Dawn had commanded Alyssa to do something useful, rather than just sit down or move over, or "tell me your name," and the younger girl complied without questioning, feeling an unexpected camaraderie with the leader as she did so.

They wrapped the sheet around the masses of severed tresses and set it off to the side as Rita snipped away at the fabric.

"What exactly am I making?" she asked, not as if she cared all that much, but just as if she were looking for conversation.

"A bed for the newbie," Dawn said, kneeling down beside her to hold the sides while she cut.

"It's kind of small," Tessa observed.

"So is she, so it doesn't matter," Dawn said seriously.

Alyssa frowned indignantly but didn't argue.

Sabrina snorted, "It looks like a dog bed."

Tessa joined Dawn in glaring at her sister. Sabrina, although slightly miffed, did not press the matter: "Whatever." She sauntered to the bookcase and selected a book, sitting haughtily down on her cot to read.

Two hours passed peacefully, with Dawn and Rita sewing the bed together, Sabrina and Ella reading, and Tessa regaling Alyssa with little bits of Barn lore.

"I've only been here a few months but, despite what you'd think, a lot goes on in this place. One time, about five weeks ago, it started raining really hard. When it rains, our walls ooze, so we'd moved everything away from the walls like you would in a tent, you know? We put everything that we could up on stilts so it wouldn't get wet. Then the power went out and we couldn't do anything about it because the candles Dawn used to use were up on the ground level and we were afraid to open the trap door in case there was any flooding, and they'd have been wet, anyway. The only flashlight we had got totally waterlogged. We had to just stumble around in the dark until the lights went back on." Tessa laughed, remembering. "In the day and a half without power we ran all the way out of food that didn't have to be cooked. Our stove runs on electricity and we were terrified there had been a downed wire near us and that the repair crew would notice the place we're hooked up to."

"And you're laughing about this?" Alyssa looked incredulous, and slightly amused, anticipating a punch line to the catastrophe. Tessa nodded, picking up on the newcomer's thoughts. "When the power finally came back on the walls were all green and slimy, and most of us were too, just from rubbing up against them." Alyssa smiled. She was pretty sure she liked this kind and quiet girl.

"Listen up!" It was Dawn, standing to stretch after her long stint of stitching on the floor. "We're playing CTM, but only after we get some stuffing in this bed. Sabrina, I want you to dig the smaller fabric scraps out of this bag. Ella, see if you can dig up a bale of straw. I think we kept a few under the outerwear boxes. Alyssa, grab that hair, it should be dry by now."

Sabrina, elbow deep in fabric scraps by now, wrinkled her nose. "You're using her *hair*? That's gross."
Dawn shrugged, holding her hand out for the bundle of what used to be Alyssa's ponytail and emptying it swiftly into the limp, floppy cover of the dog bed.

"Go shake out that sheet, Alyssa." Dawn called the younger girl to attention. "You can put it in the dirty clothes basket after you're done."
Alyssa left, carrying the now empty sheet over her shoulder as she climbed the ladder.

"She's clever for her age," Tessa said once Alyssa was out of sight.
Her sister snorted. "It's easy to be smarter than an eleven-year-old."

"Not if you are an eleven-year-old," Rita cut in, realizing that Sabrina's argument made no sense at all.

"She's weak." Dawn was next to jump in, adding her opinion to the growing cloud.

"Yeah, but we can work on that. She'll be fine in a few weeks." Tessa tried to sound optimistic but the truth was that her experience with training younger kids in physical strength did not support her statement. The debate came to an abrupt halt when the trap door opened and first Ella, then a straw bale, and finally Alyssa came down into the basement.

"OK, Ella, bring that over here and don't let it shed on the floor." Ella did her best to oblige but straw is messy stuff. Some of it landed on the floor despite her efforts. She and Rita stuffed handfuls of straw into the bed while Dawn held the top open for them.

"I do hope you're not allergic to straw." Tessa looked a bit nervous.

"I don't think so." In truth, Alyssa had never had opportunity to find out.

"I think that should do it." Dawn lowered the bulging bed to the floor and rolled out her shoulders. "Who's up for CTM?"

"What's CTM?" Alyssa whispered to Tessa.

Tessa gave her a secretive grin. "You'll see."

Before they could begin the mysterious CTM, the girls had to clean up from the stuffing project. Sabrina fetched a broom and handed the dustpan to her sister while Rita and Dawn finished sewing up the last seam in the bed.

"Alyssa." Dawn called the newcomer to attention. "Get those muffins out of the cupboard."

Alyssa remembered the careful selection Dawn had made at the supermarket and nodded, wondering why on earth Dawn wanted them.

8

"OK, Alyssa, this is how the game works." Dawn stood at the edge of the weedy field, which joined the Barn on one side and extended for about an acre total.

Dawn raised her right arm. "Ella, Sabrina and Rita over here. The rest of us get the left side."

Alyssa joined her teammates on the side closer to the barn. She was still confused, but decided to just go with it for now.

"Tessa, you're the blind. I'll be runner and Alyssa, I suppose you can be guard." Dawn pulled a ragged bandana and two plastic bags out of her back pocket. "Give me those muffins, Alyssa."

The newcomer had been wondering why she still held the box of double chocolate baked goods, and as she watched she just became more bewildered. Dawn placed one muffin in each plastic bag and sealed them tightly, handing the bandana to Tess, who obediently tied it over her own eyes.

Alyssa couldn't take it anymore. "OK. What exactly is this game?"

Tess giggled behind her blindfold. "CTM," she said happily. "Capture The Muffin."

Alyssa wasn't sure what to make of that, but she had no time to express her confusion because the other team was already approaching. Rita wore the blindfold and hung onto Ella's arm for guidance as they came forward. Dawn handed Sabrina the other muffin, explaining to Alyssa as she did so.

"Each team has a muffin hidden somewhere on their side. The blind searches for their own team's muffin, if she finds it, she has to run as fast as she can into the other team's territory."

Alyssa nodded, even though Dawn didn't pause in her explanation.

"The runner crosses the line to try and distract the blind. She can either tell her the wrong directions or move the muffin less than five feet. If the guard catches her she has to go back to her side and sit in the corner for twenty seconds. If she's on her side and tags the other team's runner, they have the same punishment. Guards can give their own team's blind advice, but cannot touch or move the muffin. The guard also cannot tell the blind where the muffin is in relation to herself, the guard, that is. Guards can't go into the other team's side under any circumstances." Dawn stopped to draw breath.

"Is that all?" Alyssa was having trouble absorbing all the rules.

"No," said Dawn, "and don't interrupt."

Alyssa refrained from pointing out that Dawn had stopped talking when she'd asked her question and listened sullenly to the rest of the explanation.

"Once the muffin is found the blind can see again, but the runner can also catch her. If the blind is tagged while she has the muffin the runner who tagged her can throw the muffin as far as she wants in any direction provided it stays on the field. The blind then puts the blindfold back on and spins around ten times before continuing her search. Do you have any questions?"

Alyssa thought she had the basic idea, but something was bothering her. "If there are three people on each team, how did you play with only five of you?"

Several of the barn dwellers looked impressed, but Dawn answered with a straight face. "The runner used to change sides when she was tagged instead of getting a timeout. It was pretty tiring."

Alyssa could imagine, but she still had one question left. "So... why do you use muffins?"

Ella smiled at the younger girl. "The winning team gets to eat them, of course."

Alyssa giggled. "That sounds like fun. So... I'm a guard, right?"

"Yes." Ella explained. "Your job is to stop Sabrina here from moving the muffin, and help her sister to find it."

Sabrina looked away, reluctant to meet Alyssa's eyes out of stubbornness. Tessa was already wearing the blindfold, but smiled at Alyssa nonetheless. That made Alyssa feel a bit better.

"OK, hide the muffins!" Dawn gave the signal to begin and Sabrina entered the other team's territory to hide the muffin. The leader did the same on the half designated to her opponents. They weren't exactly hiding the muffins. Alyssa watched as Sabrina threw her muffin to the ground in the far left corner of the field and jogged back to join the others in the middle. Dawn was more meticulous, carefully selecting a place near the middle and back of the other side.

The leader returned at an unnecessary sprint and ordered everyone into starting position. Mimicking Ella, the other guard, Alyssa went to stand about ten feet away from Tessa who had been led to the exact center of their territory by Dawn. The blind was down on her knees, ready to start groping around as soon as they were allowed to start. Both runners took up a position near the borderline, staring warily at each other as Dawn counted down to the start.

9

"...Three, two, one, GO!"

To Alyssa, it seemed as though Sabrina vanished. All of a sudden the sound of running feet registered and Alyssa struggled to throw herself after the runner.

Sabrina totally ignored her sister, fumbling around on the ground. Instead she headed to the muffin itself, bending to pick it up before Alyssa had even halved the distance between them. Sabrina tossed the muffin a few feet farther from Tessa, who by some miracle was crawling in the right direction.

"It's more to the left!" Remembering her other job, Alyssa called to the blind as she took chase of Sabrina, now sprinting for the borderline. She reached it just as Ella tagged Dawn inches from her team's muffin. The leader jogged past Alyssa, sat down in the corner of the field, and began counting aloud.

Alyssa glanced back at the blind. Tessa had passed the muffin and was feeling around a few feet behind it.

"It's behind you!" Alyssa barely had time to say it before Sabrina was bearing down on her again. This time, the newcomer was more prepared and managed to chase the runner off before she managed to get her hands on the bag.

Alyssa was breathing hard by now and she kept one eye on Sabrina, waiting for her next opportunity while she surveyed the situation on her opponents' field.

Rita was nowhere near the muffin. She was desperately trying to take advice from Ella who had to keep running off to discourage Dawn's daring attempts to move the bag. As Alyssa watched, Ella finally succeeded in tapping the leader's shoulder, running an intercept course as Dawn came in from the left. Dawn jogged back to the corner to count a second time.

Just then, everything happened at once. Ella's shouted directions to her blind were drowned out by Tessa's victory scream. All eyes were on her as she ripped off her blindfold and sprinted, muffin in hand, for the border. Sabrina had been watching her, and streaked after her sister like an ostrich. They collided inches from the borderline and Sabrina pumped her fist in the air as she flung the muffin to the farthest corner of the field. Tess pulled her bandana back over her eyes and spun around as fast as she could ten times, staggering as she resumed her search.

Alyssa was off after Sabrina but knew it was too late. The older girl was several times faster than her and had crossed the line long before Alyssa reached her. The newcomer took the opportunity to shout directions to Tessa who was now feeling her way across the far edge of the field.

"Go straight towards two o'clock!" Alyssa wasn't sure if the blind understood, she was too busy watching Rita get closer and closer to the muffin on her side. All of a sudden, Sabrina was running. She streaked towards her sister as Alyssa took chase. From somewhere far away she heard Dawn yell in exasperation as Rita took off for the borderline. Distracted, Alyssa turned to look as Sabrina reached the muffin before the blind and threw it just as Dawn caught up to Rita.

10

Back in the Barn, the losing team and the referees watched mournfully as Rita, Ella and Sabrina devoured the slightly crumbled and squished muffins.

Alyssa stroked her newly cut hair. Her head still felt strange, lighter and more vulnerable, but she was getting used to it and she was pretty sure she liked it.

"Hey, Dawn." Ella licked her fingers, savoring the chocolate that lingered there. "Can we listen to the radio?"

"Yeah!" Rita chimed in. "We haven't done that in a while."

Dawn sighed; she seemed to be in a relatively good mood. "All right, just follow the rules." "Rules?" Alyssa asked as the leader retired to her cot with a book.

Tessa, sitting next to her on a cushion, shrugged. "Basically, we can only listen to music Dawn likes or the news, and we can't have the volume over twelve."

"Dawn seems really controlling. Doesn't that get annoying?" Alyssa whispered this, as she wasn't sure the static from the storm radio Ella was trying to tune was actually loud enough to drown out her voice. Tessa shrugged, as if the thought had never occurred to her, but Sabrina, sitting behind them nodded fervently, making Alyssa jump.

"All the time, and if you ask me, she's not very good at being leader. She doesn't let us do anything."

"I wouldn't say that." Tessa scratched her head, pulling a few pine needles from her hair. "It's more like what you said earlier, Alyssa, about her being the Lieutenant Colonel of our little Barn Brigade. She makes sure we're safe and fed, even if it's sometimes a little hard on us."

"More like the evil dictator," Sabrina muttered, ignoring her sister's attempt to make light of the situation.

Just then, Ella got the radio tuned. A woman's voice came drifting out of it singing in full, resonant vibrato, filling the basement like the sail of a ship.

"Turn that *down*!" Dawn lowered her book, a collection of *Sherlock Holmes* stories with the cover falling off, and glared at the offending girl. Ella hastily killed the volume.

"Tell me more about yourselves." Alyssa demanded of the twins as soon as she could be heard over the aria on the radio.

"Our last name is Mantz." Tessa offered.

"Tessa and Sabrina Mantz? Your names are so pretty! But are you sure you should be telling me that?"

Tessa shrugged. "I don't see the harm. It's not like you're in a position to report us. And thanks for the compliment. I've always wished I'd been the one named Sabrina, but it's nice that someone likes my name."

"You don't like the name Tessa?" Alyssa was a bit surprised.

The older girl shook her head. "Nah, Tessa's alright. It's Teresa that I don't like; it sounds so stuck-up."

"I'll never understand you. Teresa is a great name." Sabrina casually examined a small scratch on her arm.

Tessa rolled her eyes. "You're not allowed to call me that," she told Alyssa. "You could get away with calling me almost anything else, but not Teresa."

"You were almost named Renata," Sabrina offered, carelessly.

"Really? They never told me that."

Sabrina's face turned spiteful, but she still didn't meet her sister's eyes. "They never told us a lot of things."

The three fell into an awkward silence just as the last notes of the soprano faded away, replaced by a man's voice. "That was *Un Moto di Gioia*, a favorite operatic piece by Mozart, sung by the budding American opera star, Janet Cromwell. Thank you, Janet, but now we have to interrupt for some important local news from the Redfield Social Services Center."

The voice changed. The new man sounded older and rather odious with a voice like the inside of an oyster, one with a lot of sand and no pearls at all.

"I'm Wallace Ruffe. I'm the director of the Redfield Social Services Center. I'm here to alert all you Redfield residents to an unfortunate incident that has transpired in our city and encourage you to keep your eyes open. A young girl by the name of Alyssa Corsson appears to have gone missing."

The Barn Brigade froze; all eyes turned on the newcomer, some accusatory, some puzzled. Alyssa was stricken. She avoided the others' eyes as a cold and slimy something began its journey to the pit of her stomach.

"She was last seen a month and a half ago, and was only reported missing last night. We are still not aware of her circumstances. There are police searching for her, but we strongly encourage any Redfield citizen who sees a girl matching her description to contact the Social Services Center immediately. Alyssa Corsson is eleven years old, five feet two inches, a hundred and five pounds, Asian American, black eyes, and waist-length black hair. Distinguishing features include a conspicuous scar on the right side of her face. Thank you so much for your concern."

Ella turned off the radio. Everyone was staring at Alyssa, curled up with her arms around her knees again. All was quiet, a distinctive, accusatory silence, laced with unspoken resentment and mistrust. Sabrina was the first to speak.

"Well, we know what this means, right? We have to get her out of here before they find *us* too."

11

Dawn's book lay forgotten on her cot, the radio still sat on the low table, and the Barn Brigade was called to council. Sitting cross-legged on cushions, the girls looked up at their leader, standing formidably in the middle of the circle.

"Were you being searched for before we picked you up?" Dawn didn't have to point at Alyssa to make it a pointed question.

"No!"

"Are you sure?"

Alyssa thought about it. Come to that, she *wasn't* sure, even though the broadcast had made it sound as though that was the case. If she had been seen at all in her weeks at the public park, she was almost positive it hadn't been by anyone working for that Wallace man. "No," she said at last, "but you can't exactly blame me for that, can you?"

"Just watch her." Sabrina looked spiteful. "Dawn will pin anything on anyone."

"No." Dawn glared at Sabrina. "I don't accuse unfairly."

Sabrina didn't wait for Dawn to turn away before rolling her eyes.

"Anyway, Alyssa…" Dawn stared her down, just as she had the night before in the supermarket. "Did it ever occur to you that your dad might contact the authorities?"

"I feel like I'm being interrogated!"

"You are," Dawn affirmed. "Now answer the question."

Alyssa could no longer deny that Dawn scared her, but she did as she was told.

"There is no way my dad was responsible for that broadcast; he's way too out of it. I'm not defending him. It's the truth."

Dawn's eyes, a clear brown, stared insistently into hers. It seemed they were almost wishing she were right.

Sabrina stood up, facing Dawn with her hands on her hips. "Why does that matter? They're looking for her now, aren't they? We'll get busted if they track us here."

"That's not going to happen." Dawn's voice was level, but her face was fierce. "I won't allow it."

"Well…" Sabrina made her case slowly, meticulously picking out the right phrases and letting them slide off her sharpened tongue. "You're right. We can't let anyone ruin our home. But the only one about to ruin it is her." She jabbed her finger at Alyssa, but kept staring at Dawn. She was locked in a fight for supremacy.

"Alyssa has done nothing wrong. There's no way we're giving up one of us, even to secure our own well-being."

"But she's *not* one of us, not yet, and she isn't going to join this little Barn Brigade of ours if she's got people after her. We could be ruined because of this; is that really what you want? Do you want to be out on the streets again? Do you want that to happen to us? Do you think that's fair? We all know what it's like, Dawn, and we know how to make *that* situation work. But the only way *this* situation is going to work is if we take her right back into Redfield and leave her at the police station."

Dawn was silent for a moment, long enough to make Alyssa frightened that she might agree.

It was time. Alyssa made her choice. Surely even this ragtag barn existence was better than what she'd faced at home. Nothing on earth could make her return to that. She stood, six inches shorter than Sabrina and quite a bit more than that for Dawn. She felt tiny, insignificant, defeatable, but she had not let all her hardships pull her down yet, and this was not going to be the exception. With all eyes on the newcomer, full of worry and doubt, she spoke. Just a single sentence, but it was enough. It had to be said. Alyssa knew what she was doing and she wasn't about to let anyone stand in her way. For a moment, she felt more powerful than Dawn, and not at all afraid.

"If you abandon me to face my old life again, I swear I'll tell the police all about this place, and how many missing, *thieving* minors are living here."

With that she turned, carefully adjusting her sweatshirt as she sat down between two stunned barn-dwellers. She folded her arms and waited for rebuttal.

None came, a moment passed, and then...

"Fine," Sabrina said, glaring at her with harsh grey eyes, "but you do know — that's blackmail."

In truth Alyssa hadn't thought of it that way, but she wasn't given time to reflect for as soon as Sabrina sat down again, Dawn took action.

"We don't know how much information the Social Services people have, and what we do next depends on what they know."

Alyssa marveled at the leader's sudden authority and commanding language.

"What we can do is initiate a defense mode, so let's do that. But don't you dare," she turned aggressively to Alyssa, the anger apparent on her face, "do anything like that again."

There was a bated silence as the newcomer did her best not to break Dawn's gaze. Finally, the leader continued. "Ella, you're with me, we'll be the first watch shift. Then the twins and then Rita and *you*." Dawn nodded at each girl in succession, landing another threatening glare on Alyssa in the process. Rita smiled at Alyssa who couldn't fathom why, but smiled back uncertainly.

Dawn continued. "Ella and I will watch until nightfall and then switch. The rest of you, turn on the radio and make sure everyone knows if something of interest comes up. Rita, I want you to gather supplies. Take Alyssa with you and get as many buckets of water as you can. We might run out. Bring it down here and then barricade the door. We won't be going out for a while."

Rita jumped to attention. "Yes ma'am!" She grabbed Alyssa by the arm and hauled her up the ladder enthusiastically.

Outside the sun was riding low over the blackening pine trees and the sky was tinted a faint, opalescent pink. A thin breeze played with Alyssa's newly chopped hair and she shivered in the fading light.

"Hold this." Rita had a cargo bucket over each arm and was holding another out to Alyssa, who took it and followed the older girl over to the pump.

"I can pump; will you hold the buckets?" Alyssa did so and watched as Rita jumped up and down, pumping enthusiastically.

Alyssa wasn't sure what to say. She'd just effectively shattered the Barn Brigade's peaceful existence and then threatened them for it. Inside, she felt like someone was pounding her with a hammer. Each time Rita brought the pump's arm down, the hammer swung at her chest, pushing her into the ground. It was all she could do to hold back tears. Finally, she found her voice.

"If it matters to you, I'm sorry." Her voice was a little too high and guilty for her liking, but at least the apology came out coherent.

"Hmm?" Rita had been staring at the sky. "Oh, you mean because you blackmailed us?"

She was so matter of fact about it that Alyssa winced.

"Yeah, it's just… I don't know…"

"That's fine, I know you don't want to be caught any more than we do. This is how it should be: if one of us is found out, so are the rest. Dawn wouldn't have abandoned you anyway; I think she's actually a nice person somewhere underneath her control freak personality."

Something about that made Alyssa a bit uncomfortable, but she let it go. "So, you guys aren't mad at me?"

Rita shrugged as she hefted the pump a few more times. "I'm not mad, and I'm pretty sure Tess and Ella won't be either. I can't say anything about the other two though."

"I wouldn't really have reported you…" Alyssa mumbled it softly as she picked up two of the buckets, staggering at their surprising weight.

"I know that." Rita's smile, usually so ridiculous, was strangely sincere. She looked into Alyssa's eyes for a moment before shrugging off her momentary somberness. "So, is there anything you're still wondering about the barn?"

Alyssa blinked; the swift change of subject was jarring. She had no idea what to expect from this girl. It was as if she totally disregarded everything that had happened in the last hour. The newcomer did her best to take it in stride, but it felt a bit weird.

"Well, yeah. How come this place has a basement? Do barns usually have basements?"

Rita stopped to open the barn door. "You'll have to ask someone else about that. I feel like Dawn told me at some point but I can't remember."

Alyssa was even more confused by this. It had become apparent that Rita was accustomed to having to deal with tough situations, but she didn't seem to be too clear about *how* to deal with them. Subsequently she seemed to be ignoring the sticky exchange that had just taken place between Dawn and Sabrina.

Rita entered the barn and led the way to the two ladders and stood between them, calling to the lookout team above, and the radio crew below.

"Hey, we're gonna lock up, so if you want to use the outhouse you should probably do that now because, you know, we might not have access to it for a while and chamber pots are smelly."

Alyssa cringed. "Did we really have to hear that last part? It's nasty. I don't want to use a chamber pot."

"Desperate times, desperate measures!" Rita said cheerfully, and went skipping back out to the outhouse with Alyssa trailing cynically behind.

All three teams took turns using the outhouse while the other two covered the posts at radio and watch duty. Finally, when everyone was done and back at their own stations Rita showed her charge how the barricade worked.

"There's a key too," she said, producing it from beneath her tee shirt, "but it only works from the outside and there's no back entrance. Dawn said she wanted to make one but we haven't gotten around to it yet. In absolute emergencies we're allowed to jump from the door in the gym. I have no idea why anyone puts a door fifteen feet from the ground, but it might come in handy someday, you never know." Rita returned to the matter at hand with a rapidity that caught Alyssa by surprise. "Anyway, we use this board to make sure no one gets in." She indicated the thick piece of wood dangling from two thin cords above the frame of the door. The cords joined together slightly above the center of the board and ran through a pulley, over a hook and down to a rusty old handle from which Rita unwrapped them with practiced deftness.

"Then... we let it down into these brackets..." She spoke haltingly as she concentrated on lowering the heavy barricade. "...And tie the cord back up." She did so and then went to the board, checking to make sure it was tightly in place.

"I tell you, we had to rob a hardware store for all of this stuff, it was awful, and those people know a lot more about security than the grocery store does, believe me."

"So you were here when Dawn made all these renovations?" Alyssa was curious. How had Dawn managed here alone?

"Most of it was Ella's idea," Rita confided as she rummaged through a stack of battered cardboard boxes. "Dawn's not exactly good with mechanics." Somehow this revelation surprised the newcomer; she had gotten the impression that Dawn was good at everything.

"Here they are!" Rita pulled a shallow box off the top of the stack and handed it to Alyssa. "The candles Dawn used before we came along. Let's bring those downstairs too, just in case."

The twins were in the basement and the radio was on, tuned to an irrelevant program about the current mayoral election campaign. Tessa was sketching lazily on an old legal pad at the table, keeping one ear turned towards the radio while her sister ignored Dawn's orders completely by reading a book on her bed.

"What time is it?" Alyssa wanted to know. She was still feeling a bit shy from her blatant blackmail attempt, but she was also incredibly hungry.

Tessa looked up sympathetically. "They just said." She pointed her pencil at the radio. "It's almost six o'clock. I think you two should start on dinner."

Alyssa had been hoping to hear just that so she pulled Rita with her to the chemistry table and began to rummage through the bottom cupboard.

"Is this all right?" Alyssa held up a can of green beans and the rest of the polenta from that morning. Tessa nodded and Rita pulled out the tomato sauce.

Cooking didn't take long, and Tessa helped them set the table while they worked. Finally Rita ascended the ladders with a plate of food each for Dawn and Ella. The rest of them sat down to eat, with the radio still going in the background.

"So," Alyssa asked when they had all begun eating, "how come this barn has a basement?"

Tessa looked at her bemusedly. "Hasn't anyone told you yet? The people who used to own this place were super paranoid; this was their storm cellar. That's why the ceiling's made of cement too. It's actually kind of ironic because their house burned down with them still inside. Dawn saw the empty place, explored it, and finally moved in. She won't tell us anything that happened to her before that though. She said something about living in a tent..." Tessa trailed off uncertainly.

Alyssa nodded and stifled a yawn, getting up to wash her plate.

Tessa took pity on her. "You look tired, just go to bed. I'll wash your dishes."

Alyssa bristled. "I'm eleven years old; I can stay awake."

Sabrina scoffed unkindly from the corner, but Tessa only smiled again; she certainly did a lot of that.

"That's not what I meant. I know how hard Dawn's workouts are at first. You'll be sore tomorrow."

"Thanks for telling me," Alyssa agreed grudgingly. She really was exhausted. "Is there anyone behind the curtain?"

"No, go ahead and change."

Alyssa didn't change; she just rooted around in the clean clothes, looking for a pair of long pants small enough to fit her. She finally settled for a pair of sweatpants with a reasonable drawstring and looked at herself in the mirror one more time before stepping out of the curtain and flopping down on her new bed with a sigh. All she wanted to do now was sleep, so she pulled the towel she'd been given as a blanket up to her chin and closed her eyes, trying to ignore the guilt that still gnawed at the back of her neck.

12

"Tell me," Ella said, narrowing her eyes at Dawn. "What do you really think of Alyssa?" Dawn turned around; she'd had her face pressed against a crack in the boards, straining to see the road in the failing light.

"She's a hotheaded, impulsive fool if she thinks she can get away with blackmailing us."

"You know what I mean, do you think she knew they're after her, or do you just not care?"

Dawn put her face back against the wall. "There's always the possibility she's acting for them."

Ella joined her at the wall, frowning.

"No way. You think they're on to us and, what, hired a girl to find out? Dawn, I'm sorry, but that's totally wacky."

Dawn shrugged. "I just don't want to rule it out, OK? But for now at least we're going to protect her; it's our only choice." Dawn looked spitefully at the faded carpets.

"What, because of the whole blackmail thing? Do you really think she'd do it?"

"No, she's too soft to pull anything that harsh on a bunch of strangers."

"Yeah, I guess."

Dawn sighed, taking her face away from the gap again. "Let's let the twins take over. It's dark."

Ella nodded and stayed put while Dawn went to get the next shift. Tessa appeared first and then her sister came up the ladder to the gym.

"How are we supposed to keep watch? It's dark out." Sabrina put her hands on her hips but Ella just shrugged.

"Don't look at me, just make sure to tell us if someone tries to set the Barn on fire, all right?"

Tessa laughed but Sabrina just rolled her eyes and snorted derisively.

After Ella left, Tessa took out her legal pad again and drew some more by the light of a small flashlight that Dawn had deemed acceptable for such a purpose.

"Just stay behind the stack of exercise stuff and don't let any light fall through the cracks." She'd made it sound like sand. Tessa smiled as she began to draw a portrait of Alyssa from memory.

An hour later, Tessa gave up on trying to faithfully render Alyssa's eyebrows and turned off the flashlight, crossing the floor to where Sabrina was leaning against the yoga ball with a defeated expression on her face. Tessa sat down next to her and put an arm around her sister's shoulders.

"This is going to be interesting, isn't it?"

13

Someone tapped Alyssa's shoulder. She didn't move, and then someone began tickling her toes, then pulling her fingers, and finally pinching her nose.

"Stop it!" She mumbled, rolling over in bed to avoid further prodding. Dawn yanked away her towel and pushed back her eyelids, staring her in the face.

"Get up, already. It's your and Rita's turn to stand guard." Alyssa groaned, but propped herself up on one elbow and started to get up.

"You see, Rita, this is what you're supposed to do." Dawn seemed to be in a pretty good mood, considering it was probably two in the morning. Alyssa blinked at her, trying to clear the haziness from her eyes. She groaned and stood up, putting a hand to the wall to steady herself.

As Dawn had observed, Rita was still in bed, holding the sleeping bag against her face as if her life depended on keeping her world black.

"For goodness sakes!" Dawn went to the buckets of water lined up against the wall by the chemistry table and dipped her thumb into the nearest one. She returned to the side of Rita's cot and deftly flicked the drops of water into the girl's exposed ear. Rita squealed and sat straight up.

"Great flying cheesecake!"

"Don't worry, you were just dreaming." Dawn seemed accustomed to this kind of response but Tessa chuckled from somewhere near the corner and Alyssa had to bite her lip to keep from cracking up.

"Come on, it's your turn on watch." Grudgingly, Rita stood up and stretched, her back cracking in a dozen different places.

"All right, I'm up." Rita turned to Alyssa and gave her a sleepy smile. "Let's go."

They climbed the ladder to the main level and the other ladder to the gym in sleepy silence, both too tired to talk.

"How do we do this?" Alyssa asked when they reached the top. It was obviously still dark out, and the wind moaning through the walls and rafters was cold and wet. Alyssa was glad for her sweatpants as she sat down opposite Rita and began what turned out to be an impromptu staring contest; more to keep each other awake than anything else.

"I really am sorry about earlier..." Alyssa said at last, filling the awkward silence.

Rita looked confused for a second, as though she'd already forgotten what Alyssa was talking about. "Oh! That? You don't have to worry about that. Here, I want to show you something. Lie down on your belly." Perplexed, and a little taken aback, Alyssa did as she was told.

"Put your arms above your head and let me grab them." Rita positioned herself with one foot on either side of Alyssa's slender body and took hold of each of her hands.

"Keep your elbows straight and close your eyes. Tell me when it hurts."

"What are you doing?" Alyssa kept her eyes closed as Rita pulled on her arms, forcing her back to arch. "Ouch! That hurts, stop." Rita let up a bit, but held the smaller girl in place, back bent and eyes closed.

"I'm counting to thirty, OK? One, two, three." She counted agonizingly slowly and Alyssa slowly found herself wishing for the end as her back cramped up and she fought increasingly hard to keep her eyes shut.

"Twenty-eight, twenty-nine, thirty!" Rita stepped forward, not letting go of Alyssa's wrists, lowering her gently to the floor.

"Now, keep your eyes closed, I'm going let go of your arms but don't let them flop, otherwise we'll have to do it again, just lower them slowly to the ground, OK?"

"OK." Alyssa felt the tension in her back release as she came closer and closer to the worn out carpet. Her chin touched down, and Rita squeezed her hands and let go. As instructed, Alyssa did not let her arms go, but consciously lowered them until they should have hit the floor, but they didn't. It was as if the battered carpet and creaky Barn boards had dematerialized, leaving her to keep bringing her arms slowly lower into nothingness... The carpet reappeared and Alyssa opened her eyes to see Rita's grinning face, staring at her in the darkness from right beyond her fingertips.

"That is so *weird!*" Alyssa rolled over and sat up. "How does it work?"

Rita shrugged, pushing herself up on one elbow. "Strange, isn't it? Do you know any body tricks like that?"

Alyssa wracked her brain; she thought she remembered something... "Put your hands into fists and press them together as hard as you can."

Rita eagerly obeyed, pressing with an intensity that Alyssa had not expected.

"You're allowed to breathe. Now count to a hundred, I'll do it too." Together, the two counted, looking like miniature wrestlers gearing up for a big match. Rita's hard-earned muscles bulged in her arms as she whispered numbers.

Alyssa wondered how long it had taken for pudgy, fun-loving Rita to become that strong, and how much she must've hated it.

"Ninety-nine, one hundred. Now," Alyssa instructed, "pull your hands apart slowly." Rita did as she was told and her eyed widened as the desired effect took place.

"They're like magnets!" she exclaimed, remembering just in time to keep her voice down. Alyssa nodded happily, pulling her own fists apart and enjoying the strange, sticky feeling that lingered around her knuckles.

"Unfortunately, that's the only one I know," Alyssa said regretfully.

"That's alright," Rita assured her, "we'll do partner gymnastics sometime soon. It's so much fun!" The last word came out in a squeal as Rita got a bit over-excited.

"Shh!" Alyssa warned her. "We don't want to wake Dawn up. She'd think we're being irresponsible."

"You've picked up on her personality fast."

Alyssa shrugged. "She's pretty predictable."

"Even so," Rita observed in a whisper, "you've got her figured out, and you're right, she'd practically flay us for messing around up here."

"What does flay mean?" Alyssa wondered aloud.

"I'm pretty sure it means to whip someone until their skin falls off."

"Eew!"

Rita nodded amiably, "I agree, it is eew. I don't think she'd actually do it but we'd better keep it down just in case."

Alyssa's eyes widened and she nodded fervently, which made Rita laugh.

The two spent the next few hours talking in whispers and laughing softly as they discovered more about each other. Alyssa learned that Rita had been diagnosed with ADD as a small child and still exhibited the symptoms, especially early in the morning, or after drinking a lot of coffee. She also learned that Rita could speak with a perfect Ugandan accent, courtesy of her foster mothers.

"I really think of them as my parents," Rita told her when Alyssa referred to them as foster parents. "I'd be a totally different person if not for them." She went silent for a moment. Alyssa remembered how upset she'd gotten in the van and laid a hand on her new friend's shoulder.

"I know what you mean. My parents encouraged me to sing. That was like, my hobby before things got all riled up. I was in choir and everything at school. Remind me to sing something for you when we're allowed to speak above ten decibels."

Rita chuckled. "OK. I wish I could sing. All I can do is dance. Do you like to dance?"

Alyssa shook her head. "I'm no good at it."

Rita grabbed her hand. "Neither am I, here, I'll show you." She stood up and pulled the newcomer to her feet. For a horrible second, Alyssa thought Rita wanted to dance with her, but then…

"You can watch from over there." She pointed to the corner with the climbing rope.

Rita struck a pose, one arm extended above her head, the other off to the side where she was leaning, one leg extended to the other side. There must've been some kind of music in her head to keep step to, but for the life of her, Alyssa could not fathom what it might be. The dance was some combination of ballet and polka, and Rita had been right, it was terrible. She swung her blonde hair around as she pivoted on one wobbly foot. She leapt gracefully and landed heavily, causing a dangerous amount of noise as she came down on the floorboards. Rita danced with her eyes closed and more than once she almost collided with one wall or another as she twirled and tripped to her own internal music. Alyssa shook her head. It really was painful to watch.

In another hour the sun began to send hazy rays of peach over the horizon and the girls' shift was almost over. Alyssa was appointed to fetch Dawn and Ella for the morning sentry duty as Rita continued the lookout job. The leader was already up, brushing her short brown hair and bringing out a box of instant oatmeal for breakfast. She just nodded when Alyssa approached her.

"Wake Ella up." Dawn ordered, sharply.

Alyssa, remembering what she had witnessed the day before, approached the older girl's bed and grabbed hold of the zipper pull on the outside of her sleeping bag. She yanked it towards her as, with the other hand, she pushed the sides of it away from the sleeping teenager. Ella moaned and shifted. Alyssa exposed her feet and suddenly she was awake.

"Stop that! I'm getting up already." Obediently, Alyssa stepped back to let Ella get up.

"Are you sore, Alyssa?" Ella rubbed her eyes and waited for a response.

Alyssa scratched her head. It had been a long night. "Soar? What's soar? How could I *be* soar?"

"You know, sore, like from the exercise?" Dawn joined the conversation, seemingly puzzled by Alyssa's cluelessness, but Alyssa's weary brain finally seemed to get the picture.

"Oh! I get it." She rolled her head around and flexed her arms, checking. "Ouch! Yes, I'd say I'm sore. I thought you meant soar, like S-O-A-R, you know, like flying?"

Dawn snorted. "I'd go to sleep now if I were you. Let Rita be on radio duty."

Alyssa was too tired to protest. Yawning, she headed for her dog bed and flopped down, not bothering to pull the towel over her.

In the next few minutes, the twins were awakened and told to finish preparing breakfast. The morning watch shift was dispatched to the gym, relieving Rita of her vigil. She appeared at the top of the ladder and practically fell down it to the room below.

"How come Alyssa gets to sleep? I was up all night too!" Sabrina just rolled her sleepy eyes and went back to setting the table but Tessa went over to her, peering into her face.

"You look totally dead," she pronounced, "you can sleep too. We'll keep listen to the radio for you."

"Thanks," Rita yawned, "I owe you one." And with that she stumbled to her cot and collapsed, her first snores erupting within seconds.

14

"WAKE UP! WAKE UP!" It was Sabrina. She had Alyssa by the shoulders and was shaking her back and forth while Tessa tried to restrain from behind.

"Don't hurt her, she's waking up." Alyssa's dark eyes opened to gaze hazily at the twins.

"Hm?"

"Oh, for goodness sake! What do you want already?" Alyssa mumbled grumpily as she sat up. Sabrina, only a few inches away glared at the newcomer with icy venom in her eyes.

"You stupid girl! You were seen! Some guy saw you in the alley. Now we're going to be caught and it's all your fault!" Alyssa could see tears of anger blossoming in Sabrina's eyes. She pretended not to notice.

"How do you know that?"

"They announced it on the bloody radio! You know they said to call in if anyone saw a girl fitting your description? Well someone did! He saw you stealing the buckets and getting into the van with us. We're totally busted! You're going to pay for this!"

Dawn and Ella appeared at the ladder. Tessa, having fetched them, came down behind them and stood sheepishly against the wall.

"Sabrina!" Dawn was deadly serious and her tone was dangerous. "Tell me what was on the radio just now. Tell me the exact wording!"

"They said 'And now for more news on the missing child, Alyssa Corsson. A girl matching her description was seen in they alley behind Medder Avenue two nights ago. Our witness reports seeing a young Asian girl with long black hair take a bucket from behind his garage. She was then seen getting into an old green van with several female juveniles. Once again, if you think you may have seen Alyssa Corsson, please do not hesitate to call us.'"

Alyssa didn't have time to wonder how Sabrina had managed to quote the program so exactly before Dawn turned on her. "You were standing in the streetlamp! It's one thing to be new; it's another to be totally clueless. That's just common sense! You've endangered all of us." Sabrina, still standing behind the leader, looked smug.

Dawn continued. "You're not in the right here! Dumping her now won't do anything and she'd just give us away." Dawn scrutinized Alyssa in distaste. "Blackmail. How dare you!"

Alyssa was not about to back down. If she'd learned one thing from her life it was how to stand her ground and make a point. She pushed herself off the bed and stood, hair practically rising in fury. "I may have been seen and they might be looking for me, but not for one minute are you to think that it's my fault. We've all faced obstacles. Isn't this just another one to overcome? Things might not be as easy as you want them to be but I'm telling you right now to look back at your own life." Here she eyed Dawn defiantly. "If it's been a bundle of fun then I'm the queen of England but you all have at least one triumph. You're here now and you're alive. Don't throw that away just because of this. We can still take control of this situation." She stopped for breath, not knowing where to go next.

Dawn looked at her, clear brown eyes full of fierce determination, and a new hint of admiration.

"You have a point. We won't give up, but that doesn't mean you aren't at fault. We have rules around here. You don't let yourself get seen, you don't blackmail your friends, and you don't make my own point before I have a chance to. I don't want to see you for a long time. Go up on lookout and stay there."

Alyssa was afraid to disobey so she scurried up the ladders and sat in the middle of the floor, head in her hands, and cried. She was still there when she heard the car drive up.

15

Alyssa froze, waiting for the vehicle to move and leave them safe, but it did not. No doors slammed but she heard the motor cut. Carefully, Alyssa wiped the tears from her eyes and crept to the wall, taking pains not to step on creaky sections of the floor.

There was a crack in the boards about at her knee level. Alyssa put her eye to it. There was no one on the road coming towards the Barn, or on the road going away from it. Parked right in front of the building itself, on the drive leading away from it, was a small red car with its doors still closed. Alyssa couldn't see the driver's face. She didn't know what Dawn would have wanted her to do, but she knew what she was going to do.

Alyssa scrambled towards the ladder as she heard the car door slam. She jumped through the trap door and landed hard on her ankle, involuntarily crying out in pain as she scooted to the other ladder. She poured herself down it to the room below where five faces stared at her in bewilderment and contempt.

"There's a car outside, parked in front of the barn." There was a moment of stunned silence, but no one asked if she was sure. Dawn stepped onto the third rung of the ladder and stuck her head cautiously up through the hole.

Even if she had been able to see around the van there would have been a wall in the way, but such obstacles did not hinder Dawn's ears and she distinctly heard voices coming from outside the barn. Sticking her hand back into the basement, Dawn grabbed hold of where she knew Sabrina's sweater was and pulled the girl up beside her.

"Hey!" Sabrina was taken by surprise and let out an indignant exclamation, only to be silenced by her leader's icy, and somewhat fearful glare. Dawn tapped her ear and Sabrina, recovering from her initial shock, turned her head to better hear the voices coming in from outside.

"There it is again. I'm telling you, there's something inside that barn."

"Yes, but the first one sounded more like a cat or something. That one was definitely a person."

Dawn dug her finger into the pressure point behind Sabrina's jaw and the other girl's eyes watered with pain. The speakers outside continued.

"I agree with you, but let's just leave it alone, OK? It's probably just a farm worker or something."

"You're kidding me. This place doesn't run anymore, otherwise I'd ask *them* for directions."

"Yeah, but there's *someone* in there, so go ahead and ask."

"I can't do that. The door's closed."

"That's why you knock, numbskull."

"You do it."

"Fine." There was a sharp rapping at the barn door. Nobody moved.

"See, no answer. I bet it was just a cat anyway."

"I'm positive I heard someone say 'hey', Cece."

Cece's voice went high and sarcastic. "So, what, you mean there's someone *hiding* in there?"

"That's exactly what I mean. It's giving me the creeps."

"Why? It's probably just some homeless guy."

"Criminals hang out in places like this."

"Where'd you hear that?"

"I… read it somewhere. I think we should call the police."

On the ladder, Dawn tensed. Behind her, Tessa stifled a gasp.

"Why, so they can laugh at you? Come on, let's go. I think I can figure out the map on the way."

"Suit yourself, but I'm calling whether you like it or not."

"Fine, but let's get in the car. It's cold out here." There were footsteps and the sound of two car doors slamming.

Dawn pushed Sabrina back down into the basement and closed the trap door as she came down herself.

"Go on, tell them what we heard."

Sabrina took a deep breath and, in a perfect imitation of Cece's voice she began recounting the conversation.

Alyssa didn't waste her chance this time around, totally forgetting how mad Sabrina was at her.

"How do you do that?" she asked. Sabrina only glared at her but Tessa answered for her sister.

"You've heard of a photographic memory?"

Alyssa nodded.

"Well, my sister has the same thing, but for sounds. But that's not really what we need to worry about right now."

Grave expressions clothed the faces of the Barn Brigade, all except for Sabrina. Her face was livid. "You are so dead, Alyssa. Why'd you have to squeal like that?"

"Shut up, Sabrina, you're at fault too. It's thanks to you they know we're not just a cat." It wasn't like Ella to come right out and be so harsh, but the rest of them put it down to the sheer dread that had invaded their minds.

"We have maybe three quarters of an hour before the police get here." Dawn fixed them all with a steady stare. "What do we do?" Dawn had never been the one to ask such questions before. She had always been the one with the plan.

"They'll have to get a warrant before they come barging in here," Rita offered, but Ella shook her head.

"It's a shabby old barn with a burned-down farmhouse. Do you really think they'd bother with a warrant?"

"No," Dawn said. "We have to make a plan. We have two options: siege or flight."

"If we stay here they'll probably catch us." Tessa looked worried.

"Yes, but they know we've got this van now so they'd track us down anyway."

"We could try to fight them off?" Alyssa asked doubtfully.

Dawn shook her head. "You are way too naïve. We may be strong but cops are another matter. We're no match for them."

"We could fortify the barn," suggested Ella, with a shrug.

Dawn nodded, "That's a good idea. Let's do that." It was unlike her to make a decision this quickly; the others noticed the unusual haste.

Sabrina blinked. "Wait, so we're staying? But that makes no sense. They'll catch us for sure."

"We've put too much work into this place to lose it." Dawn's eyes seemed to blaze. "Yes, we're staying."

"No, we're not!" Sabrina burst out. "I'm not going to let you idiots get us thrown in jail. We've got to get out of here right now before the police come." She was almost yelling and Dawn shot a nervous glance at the trap door above them, clearly wondering if Cece and her friend we still there and might hear Sabrina.

"It's all *her* fault!" Sabrina pointed a quivering finger at Alyssa. "She came here and everything started going wrong. We need to get rid of her!"

Dawn shook her head and Ella put an arm around Alyssa.

"Fine, side with her, all of you. Go on." No one moved. "What's wrong with you?" Sabrina was screaming by now, her face bright red and streaked with tears of anger and fear.

"Why do you always follow Dawn? Can't you see she doesn't care about you? All she wants is people to do her dirty work around here. She's probably planning to use you guys as a diversion so she can get away. You're all so blind!" Sabrina screamed.

"No using disabilities as insults. Go up in the gym and stay there."

"I'm *not* a two-year-old! You cannot put me on time out!"

"Oh, yes I can. I'm in charge around here. Get up there right now."

It was clearly even more aggravating to Sabrina that Dawn stayed completely calm, only her eyes betraying the anger boiling in her mind.

"You narcissistic brat! You only house us because we can do things for you. How can you live with that?"

"Sabrina, if you do not go upstairs right now I swear I will carry you up there myself."

"I'm going, I'm going! Are any of you coming with me?" She turned on the bottom rung and swept her eyes over all present. Only Tessa looked down in shame as her sister turned away from her and ascended the first ladder. She slammed the trap door on them with an awfully final bang.

16

Sabrina hadn't felt so helpless, scared and angry since the day she first saw her parents fight. She could remember every word, of course. She could have repeated it to the syllable, even six years later. Sitting in the gym their words and shrieks rang once again in her ears. Her memory was not a gift; it only bound her to the past with unbreakable ropes of sound. She pressed her hands to her ears and lowered her head, crying lightly into her lap. Why did everyone have to be so *stupid*? How could they just stand by while their lives were risked?

Sabrina clenched her fists and bit her lip, almost drawing blood. She couldn't stay here, and there was no way even Tessa could drag them back to their parents. If Alyssa's good-for-nothing dad was looking for her, how was it that their parents hadn't even *noticed* they were missing yet? Sabrina dug her thumb into the same pressure point Dawn had used earlier, not to punish herself, but just to inflict some pain on some part of this world that treated her so badly. It worked and Sabrina hissed through her teeth, pressing even harder, daring herself to go even farther.

She felt her nail break the skin and kept going, twisting her nail to draw blood. It hurt a lot and she reveled in the pain. It was a kind of relief from the other agonies around her, a way to let some of her anguish out. Involuntary tears dripped from her chin and, unable to bear it any longer, she pulled her thumb away and licked the blood from under her nail. She knew what to do.

All her life, Sabrina had guided Tessa, shown her where to go and what to do. She had been the one in charge. It might not have been this way, they might have grown up equals, but someone needed to eventually show the authority their parents lacked.

Sabrina stood up and began to pace over and over on the creaking boards of the gym, bloody thumbnail still in her mouth. She could remember every detail of the fight she'd just had with Dawn, and only now did the idea — no, the answer — occur to her. Sabrina looked at her watch, two eleven, if she started now... Sabrina turned and headed for the ladder.

Careful not to make a sound, Sabrina lifted the box of outerwear off its pile and tiptoed with it over to the trap door. Slowly she set it down, blocking the entrance to the basement and, she hoped, any sound she might make while escaping.

The barricade made a slight squeak as she raised it, but she knew from experience that this sound could not be heard from the basement. The doors opened outwards and Sabrina slipped through, still holding the cord for the barricade. She pushed the door shut behind her before allowing the cord to slip through her fingers and replace the board in its brackets.

Sabrina took off at a jog, rounding the corner to the main road just as the police car came around it the other way. Sabrina realized her mistake too late as the surprised officer swerved to avoid her. His window came down and he stuck his head out, eyebrows raised.

Sabrina thought about running, Dawn was always telling them not to give up before the battle was lost, but the last thing she wanted to do right now was follow Dawn's instructions.

The cop unbuckled his seatbelt and opened the door, stepping out onto the gravel of the drive.

"Who are you and what are you doing here?" He didn't seem to be a very professional cop, but he was still a cop and Sabrina wasn't about to mess with him any more than was strictly necessary.

"My name is Sabrina Mantz." She put out her hand for him to shake, so OK, maybe she was messing with him a little.

"And what are you doing here?" Said the cop, not taking her hand.

"I'd like to ask you the same thing." Sabrina thought she was handling this rather well, considering her face was probably still all puffy and red from crying, and she could feel her legs beginning to shake.

"I've been sent here to investigate a report of 'strange and possibly human noises coming from this barn.' Now tell me why you're here."

Sabrina shrugged. "I've been making some strange and possibly human noises in this barn."

The cop looked at her, eyebrows furrowed.

"Would you get in the car? I want to ask you a few questions."

"I'm afraid that won't be possible." Sabrina tried for a regretful expression, but overall her emotions were far too mixed up to manage anything but a pained look.

"Why not?" The cop looked genuinely puzzled.

"Because I'm running away from home and if I get in your car you'll ruin it all." It was technically the truth, but it wasn't what the officer had been expecting at all.

"Come with me." His voice had lost all pretenses of amiability and he reached forward to grab her arm. Sabrina knew better than to hit a police officer, and she had no time to step away so she let herself be maneuvered into the back seat of the squad car. It was all black metal bars and tightly closed doors. Sabrina was suddenly hit by the severity of her situation. She didn't like sitting back here; it made her feel like a criminal. *You are a criminal* said a little voice in her ear, *you steal from honest people for a living. I wouldn't call that innocent, would you?* Sabrina tried hard to get it to shut up, but the voice held too much truth to ignore. She had to bite her lip to keep from whimpering.

"Miss?" the policeman was behind the wheel again, notepad in hand and frown on his face.

"Hm?" Sabrina pretended not to be paying attention.

"Could you tell me where you live?"

"I told you, I ran away from home, I don't live anywhere."

"What about that barn?"

"I spent the night there." Once again, Sabrina managed by some inhuman feat not to lie to him. It actually sounded pretty convincing.

"And where do your parents live?"

"They don't live together. My mom lives at 6847 Ridger Drive in Blighton Valley."

"That's beyond my field of governance. Could you tell me where your father lives?"

"He lives in an apartment in downtown Redfield."

"What's the address?"

"1528 Cadley Avenue. He's in apartment 409."

"And, how old are you?"

"Fourteen."

"Why did you run away?" It didn't seem like he was asking it as a cop, more as someone who actually cared.

"My parents won't talk to each other. When they lived together they were always fighting. I mean like hitting and stuff. Then they separated and started taking out their anger on me." It was the first lie she'd told him but it wasn't hard to cover up. Her face was already red from crying and she let her eyes tear up.

"I see," said the officer, looking almost sympathetic. "So you'd rather I didn't take you to your parents? That sounds like a tricky situation. I'll take you to the Social Services Center orphanage instead, at least until we get everything sorted out."

Sabrina sniffed and nodded. Social Services was pretty bad, but it trumped being dragged back to her parents any day.

The officer put his car in gear and backed out of the Barn's driveway. Sabrina looked back at her home as the car pulled away and thought of her friends, even Dawn and Alyssa, but especially Tessa, with whom she'd shared everything from space in the womb to spare socks, truly praying that someday, she might see them again. "I'm sorry," she whispered as they drove away, "I'm so, so sorry."

17

The afternoon passed in relative silence. The tension of waiting for the police stretched thin after long hours of straining ears and rapid hearts. Ella paced, biting her lips and wiggling her toes. Dawn busied herself tidying the bookcase, cleaning the whiteboard and generally trying unsuccessfully to disguise her anxiety. Tessa wrote furiously on her legal pad. Rita gave Alyssa a back massage and a foot massage and finally a hand massage with brisk strokes of fingers as tense as the muscles they were easing.

Alyssa herself was lost in thought. She kept her eyes closed so she wouldn't have to see the faces of her new friends as they avoided her eyes and glanced quickly away as soon as she looked at them otherwise. She was left in her own space where the only clear things left to her were the objects she felt around her and the endless drone of the radio, speaking of nothing. She couldn't see or hear the people around her and that was good enough to get her away from them. She floated in her thoughts, letting things come and go as they pleased. She may have cried but nothing seemed real to her. Finally Ella broke the silence.

"I guess it's time for dinner. Are any of you hungry?"

By way of answer Dawn stood up from where she was folding the clean clothes and went to help with the cooking. Rita and Tessa moved the table and Alyssa helped them set it. Very soon the aroma of baked beans filled the barn. It was the main course.

"I'll get my sister." Tessa looked at Dawn. "If that's OK. Do you think they're gone?"

Dawn shrugged. "I don't think they ever came." Tessa went to the ladder.

"Hey! The trap door won't open."

"Yes it will. Here, let me at it." Dawn took Tessa's place on the ladder and pushed up on the trap door. "That's weird, it feels like there's something on top of it." She pushed with all her might and managed to lift the door about three inches, immediately sticking her arm through the gap to wedge it that way.

"Alyssa, you're the smallest, get over here." Alyssa did as she was told and proceeded to squeeze her arm past Dawn and through the gap that the leader was forcing open.

"I think it's a box." She announced. "I'll try to move it."

A few minutes of struggle ensued. Though the box was not heavy, the top edge of it was wedged against the barn wall and it took Alyssa a while to get it unstuck.

"...There!" With a great thrust, she finally managed to push the box away. She opened the trap door all the way, propping it against the wall.

"Your turn, Tess." Dawn rubbed her wrist and stepped aside, pulling Alyssa with her so Tessa could get up the ladder. "I'd go, but she'd probably eat me alive."

Tessa disappeared up to the main floor and Dawn descended once again into the quiet cooking of the basement.

It didn't take long for Tessa to smell a rat. It wasn't like Sabrina to hide but she checked anyway. Behind the exercise equipment was the only place to look in the gym and after she exhausted it she went back down to the main floor and checked the piles of boxes and bags for her sister. She opened the van and crawled around inside, checking in the trunk and under the seats to no avail. As a last resort she called Sabrina's name. It couldn't exactly echo in the barn, but the lack of response made it seem like there was a sort of resonance. Suddenly Tessa was worried. She felt her heart rate rise and looked to the box that had blocked the hole. Of course, there wasn't a note on it or anything but it had been put there deliberately and Tessa felt tears rise in her eyes as she realized why.

"Tess, get down here." Dawn's tone was grave and commanding. She sounded more serious than Tessa could remember. She rushed to the ladder and jumped into the room below.

"Listen!" The radio was on loud and its grim news filled the basement like a cloud.

"…A Redfield policeman in a rural area outside the city found her. He'd been called out to investigate strange noises in an abandoned barn. The minor shall remain unnamed because of her age, fourteen. Reportedly she was staying in the barn overnight after running away from home, where she lived in less than favorable circumstances. She is currently residing at the Social Services Center orphanage until a final arrangement can be worked out. It sure is a week for missing girls! Young Alyssa Corsson still has not been found, although the search continues. Once again, please telephone our office if you see a girl fitting her description."

Ella turned off the radio, and for the first time in more than twenty-four hours, total silence descended on the Barn. The baked beans steamed on the table, but nobody felt like eating. Tessa went behind the curtain. She wasn't changing; she just wanted to be alone. Curled into the corner between two laundry baskets, Tessa pulled her knees up to her chest, just like Alyssa did, put her head down, and soaked the sleeves of her sweatshirt with tears.

Tessa, for all her submission to Sabrina, her neutral opinions and her constant backwards dance to please, still knew herself better than even Sabrina did. She did not pack away some part of her personality in order to be submissive; she was submissive by nature. Without her sister, her protector, the person who'd taken care of her when her parents neglected to, who braved the darkness of the hallway to turn on the light, who pulled her away from the so-called guardians who screamed and threw things, held her in the basement while she cried and kept her alive while they lived on the streets. She didn't know how to survive without Sabrina, and suddenly she felt so alone. The world around her was caving in and pounding her into the floor.

She did not cry out. If she had they might have come to her, the Barn Brigade, put their arms around her and offered her consolation. Sabrina had been caught. There was no hope.

It did not occur to Tessa to be angry with her twin. Such a thing would have been against her values. But Tessa did wish for her, wish she were able to comfort her from a distance.

18

Eventually most of the Barn Brigade did sit down and eat. After an hour there were only two plates left on the table. No one wanted to touch Sabrina's portion, it was like a dead thing, drawing eyes and reaping tears from those around it. Tessa's meal was left uneaten as well, but it was more out of respect that it was left behind as the table was cleared and the dishes washed. The wastewater tank was getting dangerously full and the buckets dangerously empty. Ella and Rita went to fill them.

Neither spoke as they walked side by side, their shoulders almost touching on the way to the pump. Alyssa watched from the gym. She hadn't been assigned to lookout duty, but with Rita and Ella outside and Tessa behind the curtain, Alyssa didn't feel safe in the basement alone with Dawn. She lay on the ground staring up at the ceiling with its drafty rafters and missing shingles. She could just see the moon through one of these holes and it gave her comfort to know that at least this would never change.

"You OK?" Rita had her head sticking up through the hole in the floor.

Alyssa rolled over and propped herself up on one elbow. "Yeah, I'm fine I guess."

Rita nodded. "Dawn says to come down. She's taking watch duty tonight."

"What, all night? All by herself?"

Rita shrugged, "That's what it sounds like."

Alyssa slipped down the ladder, carefully avoiding putting too much weight on the ankle she'd hurt earlier.

"Are you sure you're OK?" Rita looked at her with concern, "You're limping."

"I kind of fell earlier, when the people were here, you know?"

"You should have Ella look at that — she's qualified in first aid."

The two let themselves through the trap door to find Tessa still behind the curtain, Ella back to pacing and Dawn waiting for them beside the ladder.

"I'm going on watch tonight. You guys stay down here."

"Are you sure you don't need any help?" Alyssa cocked her head with a concerned expression. Dawn's hand landed hard on her shoulder. "I'm fine. You need rest."

Secretly, Alyssa was relieved. The last thing in the world she wanted to do was stay awake to brood over the day's events, or be in close proximity to Dawn while she did. Ella, Rita and Alyssa brushed their teeth side by side and went to bed in their clothes, casting pitying glances towards the curtain behind which Tessa still hid.

Tessa herself was unaware of these glances, or even of the moment when Ella reached across Dawn's bed to switch off the light, for she had long ago run out of space for sadness and sunk into a fitful sleep.

Ella couldn't remember the last time she'd had a nightmare, and that wasn't exactly what woke her. Her watch announced the time: 2:26 a.m. Dawn's bed was still empty. She could feel the cold sleeping bag from where she lay. She reached around in the fog of her recent slumber for the cause of her wakefulness. Turning over, she felt the absence of Sabrina all too harshly. On a whim she arose, shivering in the sudden cold as her sleeping bag dropped away. The flashlight Dawn kept under her bed was missing, probably up in the gym with its owner, so Ella felt her way to the bookcase where they kept a reading light.

Clicking it on, Ella became aware that Sabrina and Dawn were not the only ones missing from their beds. Rita still snored, peacefully oblivious and Alyssa on her dog bed breathed softly along, belying the hardships life had forced upon her. Ella crept to the curtain and pulled it back, revealing the crumpled form of Tessa hunched in the corner, almost moaning in her sleep. Ella wondered if she'd be able to move her without waking her up. She fleetingly wondered where Sabrina was sleeping tonight. It made her sad.

She put her book light down on the dinner table and approached Tessa, kneeling down to thread an arm behind her neck and under her knees. Gently Ella lifted the younger girl up, careful to move slowly enough to keep her placidly asleep. They moved into the shadow of the corner and Ella softly let Tessa down onto her cot, arranging the sleeping bag around her. She took a moment to gaze down on her sleeping face, a smooth covering of a troubled mind, and appreciate the contrast between them. Shaking her head with a sad smirk, Ella picked up the book light and moved for the ladder. The garage was almost as dark as the basement but the moon was almost full and there was enough light to see by, if she let her eyes adjust. She clicked off the book light and reached for the second ladder, trying to be as silent as she could. If Dawn was asleep she didn't want to disturb her. If she was awake…

Ella turned on the ladder to pull herself over the edge. Dawn sat in the middle of the floor, both eyes fixed on Ella's face, surprise evident on her severe features. Her head was held erect, her pale neck clearly visible in the weak moonlight. In her right hand a kitchen knife quivered, frozen inches from her throat.

Ella's eyes widened, her heart sped up and she felt her head grow light as her lungs lost their breath. She didn't have to ask what Dawn was doing.

19

Ella pushed herself through the trapdoor and pulled the knife from her friend's grip, throwing it across the room.

"Don't you dare." Her voice came out choked and breathy. "You're not allowed to die."

Dawn looked down but Ella placed her hands on either side of her friend's face and pulled it up so their eyes met.

"What were you thinking?" In all her time in the Barn, with all the experiences they'd been through together, Ella had never seen Dawn cry. She did now, salty rivers erupting in a face of anguish and long-held pain. Ella pulled the dark haired girl toward her, eyes overflowing as she embraced Dawn. Dawn didn't hug her back but Ella could feel her shaking beneath her strong arms.

"What were you thinking?" she asked again. Dawn didn't seem capable of answering yet so Ella stood up and held out a hand to her. Dawn took it quaveringly, and the older girl led her over to the wall. Dawn sat trembling and Ella sat beside her, letting the leader's head rest on her shoulder. They were there for what seemed an age, Ella carefully keeping her breathing steady and rubbing Dawn's back, not letting her curiosity overcome her duty to help her friend.

"I'm… I'm sorry." Dawn finally said, not lifting her head off Ella's shoulder.

"I know." Ella squeezed Dawn's shoulders.

"No, you don't!" Her sobs reached new heights. Ella shook her head. Empty comfort wasn't the way to go in this situation.

"You're right. I don't know. Will you tell me?"

Dawn gasped for air, "It's my fault! All my fault! I don't deserve to live."

"That's not true!" Ella grit her teeth and patted Dawn's back.

"Yes it is!" Dawn pulled away from her and stood up, blocking the weak moonlight with her body. She was shaking.

"Shh, Dawn, you're a good person. You've kept us alive all this time. If it weren't for you we'd be living in the gutter or who knows where."

"I *should* live in a gutter!"

"No, and you shouldn't live in a Barn either, none of us should have to be here, but you sure know how to make the best of it." Ella stood up. "How long were you sitting there with that knife?"

"On-only a few minutes." So that was what had woken her up. Dawn must've been downstairs looking in the chemistry table for a weapon. Ella shivered.

"Why?"

Dawn glared at her. "It's… it's hard. I guess you wouldn't know but it's really hard. I've tried before, you know but I just can't…. I'm not brave enough!" She stomped her foot in angry frustration.

"No, I meant why did you even try? You've got a good life, Dawn." She seemed stricken and it took a moment for her to answer.

"You… you have no idea."

"I know. Please tell me."

"I can't!" Dawn screamed and the shadowy Barn shivered with its hopeless sound.

Ella was beginning to lose patience but she felt that Dawn needed her to coax whatever it was out of her so she pulled her friend to the wall again and sat beside her, stroking her hair like a mother would.

"Yes you can. You're strong."

"N-not the way you mean. I'm just s-so stupid."

"Yes, you tried to kill my friend." It took a moment for Dawn to understand but then she put her head down and covered it with her arms. It was difficult for Ella to discern her next words but their painful meaning rang clearly in her heart.

"I'm not your friend. I'm - I'm…"

"But I'm yours." Ella cut her off, and Dawn cried ever harder into her knees.

"Why? Why would you want to be my friend? I'm just, just a ruthless dictator who only cares about herself."

Ella bit her lip. "You shouldn't listen to Sabrina, she's only…" Ella didn't know what Sabrina was but she wasn't sure she wanted to.

"Only right!" Dawn straightened up and snapped her head back, smashing it viciously against the wall.

"Don't hurt yourself, please, Dawn."

"Why not? I deserve a thousand more than that."

"No, you haven't done anything that bad."

"You don't know the half of it."

"Then tell me." Dawn closed her eyes and took a deep breath, only to double over again with increased sobs.

"Shh—" Ella stopped herself just before she said "it's OK." She knew it wasn't true and it would only make matters worse. Dawn began to rock. Back and forth over and over, tears dripping onto the ground around her.

"I'm trying, I swear I'm trying, this is… really hard." Ella's eyes slid to the knife, lying in the corner. She nodded.

"Can I do anything to help?" It was all she could think to say and an honest wish as well, but Dawn just shook her head and Ella fell silent.

They stayed there, Dawn curled into a ball against the wall and Ella beside her, patting her back and holding her as her sobs slowly abated and she was able to raise her head.

"I n-never told you about how I got here. Anything I hinted was probably a lie."

"I know." Ella hugged her more tightly.

"I h-had a p-pretty good life until I w-was twelve." Another wave of tears overcame her and once again she tried to bang her head on the wall but Ella saw it coming this time and put her hand up to stop the blow.

"Ouch!" Ella had to try hard not to swear as her fingers were caught between the splintery barn wall and Dawn's skull. "Careful, I don't want you to hurt either of us."

Dawn shook her head, took a hiccupping breath and continued. "I lived with my p-parents and my l-little br-" her words were obscured as she dissolved into tears again.

"You have a little brother?"

"Y-yes." But Dawn was shaking her head. She didn't look up as she kept going.

"My dad…" The rest of her sentence was lost and Ella held her breath as Dawn tried again.

"My dad k-k-killed himself."

Ella wasn't surprised. "Oh, Dawn." She laid a hand on Dawn's head. "I'm sorry."

Dawn shifted, wiping the tears from her chin and glaring at the floor in front of her.

"And so you ran away?" Ella knew she wasn't right but Dawn needed a prompt and that was the first one she found.

"No. I n-never r-ran away." That didn't make sense, but Ella knew she might have misheard.

"We were fine, fine!" Dawn banged her fist against her shin. "But then…" She was overcome again and Ella began to hum, not really a song, but just something to comfort herself, and hopefully Dawn as well.

"Then she, my m-mom, she set the... set the..." Dawn began to rock again, sobbing audibly and clenching her fists.

"She set the house on fire!" Dawn chocked and coughed.

"I'm sorry," Ella said, "But why the hell would she do that?"

Dawn shook her head. "I d-don't know. I n-never saw her again."

"Then how do you know she set the house on fire? Couldn't it have been, you know, an accident?"

Dawn shuddered. "I s-saw her d-do the garage."

Ella sighed sympathetically and let her own head rest on top of Dawn's. "I'm so sorry," she said at last. It sounded hollow, but it was the truth, so she said it again, "I'm so, so sorry."

"We were asleep. She must have snuck out and run away after, after she did it." Dawn paused and closed her eyes. "I woke up and the curtains were on fire and I could hear the fire on the other side of my door." Ella nodded; she'd heard that a fire of that volume could sound just like a wild animal. Dawn took a deep breath, gathering herself, and when she spoke her voice was level and, although she did not look at Ella, she reached up to grab her hand.

"My brother was screaming in the next room. I heard him calling for help." Dawn squeezed Ella's hand, it was the same one she'd banged against the wall, Ella winced, but Dawn didn't notice. Her eyes were still closed.

"I tried to open the door but it was stuck, so I..." She paused and swallowed, forcing herself to continue. "I took the blanket off my bed and jumped out the window." Ella did try to suppress her disbelief but it didn't work too well.

"I thought you said the curtains were on fire." Dawn nodded.

" The window was open. She had taken off the screen and set my curtains on fire."

"How did you get past them?"

90

"I held the blanket over my head. My bedroom was on the ground floor so I landed on the grass." She took a deep, if shaky breath, letting it fill her and holding it awhile.

"I ran for the garage. She was still there, putting boxes in the car, things she thought were m-more important than her children." Dawn's lip quivered and she bit it, almost piercing the skin. "She never saw me watching. She drove away and set the garage on fire too. I went back to the house, I ran around it five times, but my brother wasn't there." Another tear followed a beaten track down her check. "I called his name, I went to his window but I couldn't see anything but fire." Dawn's strong shoulders shook with a sob and her voice broke. "I went to our barn."

Ella gasped. "You lived here? That was your house?"

Dawn sighed. "Yes. I didn't have a phone to call the fire department and they'd have been too late anyway. I tried pouring water from the pump over it, but it was hopeless." Dawn shook her head. "I waited in the Barn for two days. I stayed in the storm cellar until I was sure the ashes were cold."

"You must've gotten so hungry." It was a strange thing to think, it seemed so mundane, but Dawn shook her head.

"I didn't want to eat. I didn't really want to do anything. Eventually I went out and looked around. Ella, there was nothing left. Nothing. Just a big pile of burnt ashes in a hole. There wasn't a basement, so everything just kind of collapsed."

Ella rubbed her broad thumb over Dawn's fingers.

"I didn't want to look, but I had to. Everything was gone and I had to know if he was still there."

Ella didn't want to hear the rest, she didn't want to know what Dawn had seen in the ruins of her home, but it felt like something she owed her friend. Dawn had had to live it, so the least Ella could do was hear her out, crying a little herself.

"It had rained since the fire and the whole thing smelled terrible, sour almost. I poked around with a stick for a while and finally…" Dawn broke down again and put her head in her hands, pulling away from Ella.

"I found him, Ella. But there were only b-bones. I let him die, I could have saved him, but I left him there." She shuddered and folded onto herself. Ella didn't know what to say; she could only cry harder and pull Dawn against her ever more tightly. Dawn said no more, letting the silence stretch long with reflected shadows of memory and regret. At last, Ella found her voice.

"What was his name?"

Dawn turned to her, her eyes just catching a sliver of moonlight from the missing shingle.

"Eric." Dawn realized she hadn't spoken the name in years. That thought pulled at her heart and she reached for Ella, hugging her back for the first time since she'd thrown the knife away.

"Thank you." Dawn spoke into Ella's sweater and felt Ella nod in acknowledgement.

In her own mind, Ella thought she knew why Dawn had chosen tonight to tell her long-kept secret. Sabrina had left Tessa behind, just the way she'd left Eric, if not exactly to the same fate. They were too much alike. They'd both abandoned someone they loved to save their own lives, but Dawn had ended here, living almost comfortably in a barn. And where was Sabrina? She was stuck in a room at the orphanage, waiting for her fate to fall, and any way it fell, it wouldn't land on the grass. She wouldn't tell Dawn that. Her friend had been through way too much tonight to risk psychoanalyzing her. Instead, she whispered in Dawn's ear, "I think you're amazing. You're so brave."

"So are you." Dawn pulled back and kissed Ella's forehead, almost like a blessing. "You're a wonderful friend."

"Thanks."

20

Sabrina stared at the wall and tried not to think. Any way she turned there was another wall, another reason to beat herself up. There were other girls in the dorm; Sabrina had been put in with the first vacancy and quickly met Leann, Brooke, and Gabby.

None of them had spoken since the social worker left. Leann and Brooke lay on Brooke's bed and paged idly through a fashion magazine. Sabrina couldn't see what Gabby was doing on the bunk above her, and didn't particularly care. They were all a few years younger than her and seemed painfully akin to Alyssa whenever she caught any of their eyes.

The room was spare — only two bunk beds, two dressers and a small shelf of personal items. The bottom shelf was empty, meant for the girl who occupied the bed Sabrina was now lying on. It felt weird, like she wasn't even there. She turned over and looked at the wall, at the bumpy white paint marred with cracks and the subtle shadow of her own body, cast by the flickering fluorescent light. Her watch said it was only four o'clock. It could have been days later and she wouldn't have known. But she did care. The police were probably busting the Barn Brigade right now and she had abandoned them, abandoned Tessa to that fate.

She scratched restlessly at the thin mattress. When Sabrina rolled over again she was met by an upside down face dangling off the upper bunk, surrounded by a shower of bright red hair that came down at least a foot and a half below her scalp.

"Hiya!" Gabby seemed almost cheerful. Sabrina wondered why. There was nothing she could see to be happy about; then again she had just run away from everything she cared about. She decided to give Gabby a chance.

"Hey, what are you doing?" Sabrina asked.

The redhead grinned and her hands appeared on either side of her head, gathering her hair into a ponytail on top of her head. "Making an Ancient Poodle."

Sabrina squinted at her. "*What?*"

"An Ancient Poodle hairdo, like this." She snapped a hair binder from her wrist and twisted her mane into a crazy Dr. Seuss look.

"Can I it see the right way up?" Sabrina didn't actually care, but it seemed the polite thing to say. The hairdo bobbled as Gabby nodded; then she grabbed the slats of her own bed and swung her legs over until she was sitting on the lower bunk beside Sabrina.

"That was kind of impressive." Sabrina could have easily done the same, but Gabby was younger and seemed inclined to be praised. As if to prove Sabrina's point, Gabby giggled and poked the Ancient Poodle. The hairdo now looked like a slightly wobbly orange doughnut with a tail. Sabrina gave a sarcastic thumbs up.

There was a knock at the door and an aide appeared with a pile of bed sheets under one arm.

"Oh, hello there, you're new, aren't you?" Sabrina nodded and the aide set the sheets down next to her. "My name's Tori — I work here. It's nice to see you're getting along with Gabby. I hope you'll settle in well." She left with a small wave and Sabrina shooed the younger girl off her bed so she could put the sheets on. In her head she was already wondering how she could escape.

21

The Barn Brigade never ate breakfast that morning. Ella and Dawn had stayed in the gym until daybreak, talking and crying and even laughing at times. When they were finally able to see each other clearly, Ella picked up the knife that lay forgotten in the corner and led the way downstairs. To no one's surprise, Tessa was already awake, brushing her teeth at the sink. She looked faintly puzzled to see them, but said nothing.

Dawn went behind the curtain and changed into a pair of yoga pants and a T-shirt. Ella was already dressed, so she woke Alyssa and Rita with drops of water in their ears and waited as they roused themselves.

"Good morning," Alyssa muttered. There was no answer. She didn't really expect one. Ella took the cushions from beneath the table and arranged them in a circle on the floor, all six in an unspoken tribute to Sabrina. Rita didn't have to be told what to do. As soon as she was dressed she sat down on her usual cushion and waited, back straight and eyes wide. Tessa joined her shortly and soon after that Alyssa emerged from the curtain and sat down beside them. Ella and Dawn stood in the corner by the ladder; Ella held Dawn's hand and pushed her gently into the circle, sitting down behind her.

This whole setting seemed to Alyssa strangely reminiscent of a courtroom, as if they were the jury and Dawn the defendant. All of them could see her shaking, but she did not cry. She had used up all her tears in the darkness of the gym and now she was as ready as she ever would be.

"I want to tell you a story." She began with her eyes shut, turning slowly on the spot so everyone could see her. Alyssa felt her pulse begin to beat in her neck. Her university sweatshirt suddenly felt too hot and her breath was shallow, like someone was squeezing her lungs. She realized she was scared of what Dawn might say, but she bit her lip and looked up to the leader's face, awaiting the suspect's plea.

"I've lived here my whole life. The house that burned down was mine." Dawn was expecting some expression of surprise from the group, but all were silent. She opened an eye to look at Ella. The older girl gave her a tiny nod and Dawn went on. She told the Barn Brigade everything she'd told Ella the night before, and went on, explaining her self-loathing and regret.

"I guess I knew what Sabrina did was wrong, leaving us, only to get herself caught. I despised her for it, but I didn't want to admit how similar we were." She turned to Tessa. "I left Eric to die, and she left you here to be caught by the police, only she was the one who got caught. Even if she didn't mean it like that, it was a huge sacrifice. I didn't give up anything for Eric. He didn't deserve to be burned alive by his own mom." Her face had gone from cold despair to livid anger and she glared into space as she finished.

"I thought I'd never be able to live it down, to move on, so last night I... I..." She turned to Ella for help but Ella shook her head.

"Go on, you can tell them." Dawn swallowed and stared at the ground. Alyssa found that her heart was racing again. What had Dawn done? Possibilities raced through her mind, but none of them seemed quite horrible enough. Dawn squeezed her eyes shut and tilted her head to the ceiling.

"I tried to slit my throat." Alyssa gasped audibly and everyone looked at her.

"I stopped her." Ella patted the newcomer's shoulder. Dawn let out a deep breath and smiled falteringly at Ella.

"I really just want to apologize. I've been a total control freak and a really bad leader. I don't want you... us... I don't want the Barn Brigade to be a dictatorship." Tessa's lip quivered, but Dawn didn't notice, she was looking at the floor.

"I know I shouldn't be so dominating and unyielding and selfish. I'm sorry I've been such a bad... a bad I don't know, Lieutenant General? Anyway, I don't want that title. I won't blame you guys at all if you don't forgive me, but I'd like to know, either way, OK?"

Dawn held her breath, eyes closed. Behind her, Tessa felt something settle in her heart, something that had been floating uncomfortably, unfixed and painful since Sabrina's departure. It found its place and she stood, her face blank and set. She placed a hand on Dawn's shoulder and turned her around. Startled, the older girl turned, looking straight into Tessa's gray-eyed stare. They faced each other, communicating on a level beyond speech, an understanding reached; Tessa raised her hand and slapped it quickly across Dawn's face.

The leader's cheek didn't have time to turn red before Tessa's arms were around her and she was sobbing into Dawn's shoulder. She had never hugged Dawn before, she was sturdy, not like Alyssa who looked like she'd break if you touched her, and not like Ella, with her slight chub, more like Sabrina, slim and wiry. Thinking this Tessa squeezed tighter and she felt Dawn's arms wrap around her back, and then more arms as Rita joined and more with Ella and Alyssa. They stood there, on the dirt floor of a ramshackle barn in the middle of nowhere, quite at home.

22

Rita and Ella led the proceedings. With faces still damp from tears the Barn Brigade assembled before the whiteboard.

"I've spent the most time in the orphanage of all of us." Rita held up a marker. "I'll draw a map." Ella nodded and Rita set to work.

"We need to rescue Sabrina." Ella didn't particularly like stating the obvious, but it was a place to start. "Anyone have a plan?"

Three blank faces stared at her. She tried hard not to lose her resolve.

"Right. Well, let's start by taking an inventory of what we could do."

"We could break in..." Alyssa felt a compulsion to contribute something and even though she knew this wasn't a good idea she said it anyway.

Ella shook her head. "I'm afraid they'll have better security than the super market. Children are sometimes considered to be worth more than vegetables."

Alyssa nodded, relieved that she wouldn't be held accountable for their failure.

"We could do a full scale jail break." Tessa sounded doubtful and Ella confirmed her doubts with a shake of the head.

"No, that would be on the news and the last thing we want is a ton of kids on our hands when we're trying to run from the police."

Tessa shrugged and settled herself onto the cushion more comfortably.

"How about we turn ourselves in and then break out?" Dawn suggested.

Ella had to think about that one. "There's still the danger of being on the news, but I'll take that as possibility number one." Dawn looked gratified and Ella took over the whiteboard to write it down.

"Hey, uh Rita? Is that the ground floor or the first floor? I can't tell." Alyssa squinted at the map Rita was drawing without success.

"It's the first floor, that's where the dorm rooms are." She pointed to what seemed to be a hallway with little rooms coming off it. "I think this is the girls' wing."

"You think?" Dawn sounded more amused than usual, although her raised eyebrow was the same as ever.

"It might also be the boys, I can't remember which is which."

"So, we might infiltrate to wrong dormitory by mistake?" Alyssa grimaced, drawing an uncharacteristic giggle from Dawn.

"Anyway," Ella continued, "we've got a friend to rescue, have you guys got any more ideas?'

"You and I could pose as... as... OK, scratch that, I don't know what we could pose as." Dawn chuckled. "I guess I'm being kinda useless where this is concerned."

"Well, it's another theory, we could pose as... OK, I have no idea either." Ella rolled her eyes guiltily.

"We have got something to our advantage." Tessa looked up from where she'd been lying on the floor with her head on her cushion. "You're technically an adult, Ella. What could we do with that?"

Ella looked surprised and Tessa snickered at her bewilderment. "Well, I guess I could… pretend to ask for a job… wait, no… that's too risky. How about an internship?"

"Yeah! You could work on the night shift and — "

"And sneak her out to us!" Rita rubbed her hands together. "That way we wouldn't have to worry about breaking into the wrong wing."

"Great!" Ella smiled tightly. "Now we just have to work out exactly how to make this insane plan work."

23

Several hours later, Ella pinned their newly formed plan to the wall with a sigh. Though they had managed to come up with a plan, it was an extremely fragile one and none of them were thrilled with the results.

Dawn cracked her neck and yawned, standing up at long last from her cushion. "I'm going to take a nap. Would you guys mind making lunch without me?" The others agreed wholeheartedly and Dawn collapsed onto her cot and was asleep within minutes.

"That's unusual." Tessa glanced at their sleeping leader. "She's usually a total insomniac."

"She was up all night, in case you've forgotten." Ella gave her a mock reprimanding look.

"I suppose." Tessa nodded sympathetically and went to wash her hands.

Rita pulled cans out of the cupboard. Tomato soup and Spaghetti-O's. "Which one should we have?"

Alyssa looked up from setting the table and pointed to the soup.

"I'm on it!" Rita's skills with a can opener were mediocre at best but she managed to get enough of a hole in it to pour out the gloppy canned soup into the tarnished saucepan. She examined the label on the can and turned the stove on.

"Tess, could you help me back here?" Ella was now behind the curtain sorting through the basket of clean clothes. Tessa nodded and joined her.

"What do you need?"

"Can you go through all of this and take everything that will fit me and put it in a pile right here?"

"OK, but what exactly are you doing?"

"Looking for something to wear to a job interview."

"You think we'll find something like that here?"

Ella hesitated. "Well, no. But we've got to look before we go running off to steal something."

"You're right, I guess." Tessa knelt next to her and pulled a bundle of shirts out of the basket. Because of Ella's height the only person who could share her clothes was Dawn, and owing to their significant structural differences, these exchanges could only go one way. As a result, Ella almost had a wardrobe all to herself, but almost everything in it had been swiped from the Salvation Army parking lot and wasn't in the best condition.

"Would this work?" Tessa held up a plain black shirt with a slight V-neck and Ella pursed her lips, considering.

"Yeah, I guess so. Are there any pants to go with it?" They both went back to rummaging but still had not found anything by the time Alyssa called them for lunch.

"What are you doing back there anyway?" Alyssa asked as she filled the plastic cups with water. Tessa explained and Rita joined them at the table, setting the pot of soup down between them.

"It's no use," Rita said with an overly dubious expression on her face.

"You're awfully cynical today," Alyssa observed with her mouth full.

"It's for your own good," Rita exclaimed, looking as if this should be totally obvious. "If we have to go get Ella more pants, we can get you something that fits while we're there."

"That's true," Ella remarked eyeing Alyssa's apparel. "It would be different if you could wear the twins' stuff, but even that's too big." Alyssa was wearing a pair of sweatpants rolled five times at the waist and three at the cuffs and a huge T-shirt bearing the legend *three rights make a left*.

"Don't rub it in." The youngest member of the Barn Brigade pretended to sulk until another question occurred to her. "Hey, how come there aren't any boys around here? I mean, isn't it a bit odd that no boys ever came along?"

"I don't know about the official statistics," Ella began, "but I'm pretty sure there are about twice as many female runaways as there are male. At least at our age."

"It's funny how you say 'our' age, when you're actually eight years older than me."

"Yeah, it is. But you could be a lot more immature than you are, and that's a compliment."

"Thanks." Alyssa smiled to herself. It felt good to get an honest compliment at last.

24

Sabrina held onto Gabby's shirt and tried not to trip as she was pulled through the building. They passed a rather ugly painting of a man with a big nose and rounded the corner, skidding to a halt before a door marked simply 'Office'.

"What's in here again?" Sabrina asked as the excitable twelve-year-old hopped up and down.

"The storage room."

"Then why does it say 'Office'?"

Gabby shrugged and put the key they'd gotten from the supervisor into the lock. Sabrina's first thought when the door swung open was, *in which century was this an office?*

It wasn't even possible to step in. Everything was arranged on shelves that ran from the floor to the ceiling.

"Here," Gabby thrust a box at Sabrina, "Pick a toothbrush." Taken aback, Sabrina did as she was told.

"You also get your own hairbrush, but we all share shampoo."

"Thanks." Sabrina picked up one of the cheap plastic brushes and looked forward to the next morning when, if she still hadn't come up with an escape strategy, this brush would probably be defeated by her hair.

"What else do I need?" she asked. Gabby placed a hand on her shoulder to push her to her knees.

"What are you doing? Get off!"

"Stand still. I'm getting on your shoulders. How else do you expect me to reach the top shelf?" Sabrina sighed and let the redhead climb onto her back, waiting until she was secure before standing up.

"Here's a washcloth, some deodorant and some dental floss. That should be enough for now."

"OK." Sabrina started to get to her knees so Gabby could get off, but the younger girl grabbed hold of her stubby pigtails and hooked her feet around Sabrina's back. "Can I stay up here?"

Sabrina sighed and got carefully to her feet, closing the 'Office' door behind them and turning the key to lock it once more.

25

Ella and Tessa dug their way through the entire Barn Brigade's wardrobe and the only thing that might have worked was almost five sizes too small for Ella.

Tessa knelt back on her heels and sighed. "Oh well, at least this way Alyssa'll get something decent to wear." Ella reluctantly agreed and helped the younger girl to pile all the clothes back into the basket.

They traipsed out from behind the curtain to find Rita and Alyssa just finishing the dishes.

"Hiya!" Rita waved a soapy spoon in the air.

"Hiya!" Tessa repeated and Alyssa turned to Rita looking defeated.

"I'll finish the rest, I guess," said Alyssa.

Ella raised her eyebrows. "Were you betting on something?"

"Yup!" Rita had a slightly evil grin on her face. "I bet her the rest of the dishes that one of you would repeat 'hiya' if I said it."

"In that case," Tessa said, rolling up her sleeves, "I'll help with these." She took up a position to rinse and Alyssa looked at her gratefully.

"So, we'll exercise after you guys are done?" Ella inquired.

Alyssa's shoulders slumped, but Tessa agreed and so Ella and Rita disappeared to the gym to set up.

"Don't worry," Tessa told Alyssa once they were gone, "it'll be better than before. Are you still sore?"

"Yeah," Alyssa grumbled, "and I hurt my ankle falling down the ladder to tell you about the stupid car people."

"You mean Cece and her boyfriend?"

"Yes, the stupid car people!"

Tessa shook her head, chuckling. "OK, they can be the stupid car people."

"Good," Alyssa said, satisfied.

They finished the dishes in amiable conversation and then Tessa turned to Dawn.

"You think we should wake her up?" Tessa asked. "She'd probably want to exercise with us."

"I think we should let her sleep. She's had a long night and a stressful day." The truth was that Alyssa wasn't quite sure where she stood with the new Dawn. Though the leader had been very agreeable during the planning that morning, Alyssa still didn't know if she had to be on her toes or not.

"OK, I guess you're right. She does need the rest. But let's leave her a note so if she wakes up she'll know we haven't been kidnapped." Tessa went to the whiteboard and took a piece of school chalk from the bin underneath it.

"What's that for?" Alyssa asked as Tessa went to the side of Dawn's bed and began to write on the wall.

"I keep forgetting you're new," Tessa whispered. "This is how we leave messages for each other. We wash it off afterward, but these cinderblocks are excellent for writing on, just like sidewalk."

Tessa finished and replaced the chalk. Her message read simply, *upstairs*.

Alyssa frowned, "Is that all you're going to write?"

Tessa looked uncomfortable. "I can't spell the word *exercise*." she confessed, and Alyssa smirked. "Neither can I."

They ascended the ladders one by one and arrived on the upper floor to see Rita and Ella sitting on the floor with their fists pressed together, counting very slowly. Tessa looked confused, but Alyssa grinned and Rita winked at her.

"OK, now try to pull them apart." They'd reached one hundred and Ella did as she was told, testing the strange magnet-like connection between her hands with suspicion.

"That is so weird!" She shook her hands out vigorously and stood up. "Alyssa showed you that?" Rita nodded and gave Alyssa a high five.

"OK, let's do weights today." Tessa sounded far too enthusiastic.

Alyssa shrank back but Ella noticed and grabbed her arm.

"You get the smallest ones, don't worry." Ella said. "We don't even have a barbell or anything intimidating like that, it's only these tiny ones." Ella pointed to a small assortment of hand weights. "You can have the two pound ones."

"OK." Alyssa was still doubtful, but she lifted the weights and they didn't seem too horrendously heavy. Tessa and Rita both took five pound weights and Ella took a pair of eight pound ones.

"Line up!" The oldest girl got in front of them and held her weights out to either side, indicating the amount of space they should have.

The workout wasn't at all what Alyssa had expected. Ella led them through a series of repetitive movements, none of which involved pumping arms above the head, or squatting like a sumo wrestler. About halfway through her muscles began to scream, even with only four pounds total; it was hard work. They ended with a minute and a half of arm circles, still holding the weights. Alyssa thought she might die.

"Who's first on the rope?" Ella asked, and Rita waved her arm in the air. Alyssa wondered if she could climb. Her own arms felt as if they'd never work properly again.

Rita went to the rope. It had no knots in it like those Alyssa was used to seeing and the blonde climbed it in a way she'd never seen. First she wrapped her right leg around it, then trapped the rope between her feet. She reached up and pulled, elevating herself about two feet and trapped the rope again. Tessa saw Alyssa's surprise and took the opportunity to explain.

"That's how they climb silks in the circus. Ella did a circus summer camp when she was in fourth grade."

Rita began to come down, bending her knees then releasing her feet and seeking a lower grip.

Tessa was next; she pulled herself up in much the same manner and touched the ceiling before coming down.

Ella was likewise swift, belying her bulky form with an unexpected grace. Alyssa cowered as Ella came back down and turned to her victim. Seeing her expression, the older girl laughed.

"Get over here, I'll teach you." Alyssa let herself be ushered to the rope.

"You saw how we did it, right? Wrap your leg like that." Alyssa put the rope against the outside of her right thigh and wrapped.

"You've got it on the wrong side." Ella corrected her wrap with the rope hitting the inside of her leg first then spiraling down to rest on top of her bare foot.

"OK, now get a good grip above your head, and pull." Alyssa's muscles were already dead, but she did as she was told, floundering her legs to recover the wrap, which had slipped off as she'd moved upward. Ella helped her and pushed her feet together around the rope.

"Ouch!"

"It hurts, doesn't it?" This was not the type of encouragement Alyssa had been seeking. The rope's rough weave pressed into her feet, pinching them and squishing them.

"Do you think you can do another?" Ella asked. In truth, Alyssa doubted it but thought she'd better try, so she nodded.

"Right answer!" Ella grinned. "Your mind always gives up before your body does. That's Dawn's line, by the way."

Alyssa reached her protesting arms above her head and gripped, pulling upwards and fumbling to step on the rope again. This time she didn't pause; she just reached up again and forced herself to do another. On the fourth try her arms gave out and she dangled from only her hands, her shoulders being pulled out of their sockets.

"Just let go — I'll catch you." Alyssa might have doubted Ella's words, hung on longer, or hesitated to work up her nerve, but she simply wasn't able to. Her fingers slipped off the rope and she fell into Ella's arms.

"That," Ella told her, "was incredible for a first attempt. Are you sure you've never done this before?" Alyssa nodded and wiped sweat from her neck.

"In any case," Tessa piped up, "let's go downstairs."

Dawn was still asleep and Rita sponged the message off the wall, careful not to wake her.

"What are we doing for tutorial?" Tessa asked, turning to the whiteboard.

"Your choice," Ella replied, sitting down on a cushion. Alyssa sat down next to her.

"You rotate teachers?" Alyssa cocked her head and Rita nodded, getting comfortable on Ella's other side.

"It's usually Ella," Rita jabbed a thumb at her companion, "because she's had the most education, but the rest of us know some things she doesn't."

"For example..." Tessa turned the whiteboard around to the other side, "I went to a French immersion preschool."

On the whiteboard that now faced them was written something Alyssa could not comprehend.

Tessa pointed to the words for Alyssa. "*Nous*," she indicated the group on them, "*habitons dans une grange.*" She pointed to the walls. Alyssa hadn't the faintest idea what she was talking about. The lesson went on for about forty-five minutes, during which Alyssa learned how to say one sentence: *Je ne comprend pas.*

Dawn awoke soon after they'd finished and was informed of all that had happened during her nap.

"I guess that means we're going into Blighton Valley tonight." She grimaced. "if we're seen now, it's all over."

26

Dinner had been eaten and cleaned up, the outhouse had been visited and the wastewater tank was empty. Everyone was asleep at midnight when the alarm clock went off. Dawn stretched and roused the others in her routine way. There was a certain amount of yawning as the girls got dressed in plain black clothes and grabbed black burglar bags. Once in the van, Rita showed Alyssa the trick.

"See, the Salvation Army has security cameras. But all you have to do is avoid being caught on them." She pulled a small pouch out of the burglar bag and thrust it in Alyssa's face. "We sneak up behind their range of vision and put these over the cameras. That way if anyone looks over the video tape, it'll just look like the systems need maintenance."

"That's smart." Alyssa was impressed. "So, how are we getting in this time?" It was Dawn who answered her.

"There's an alarm on the front door, but we can pick the lock of the employees' door, no problem." The van passed a sign welcoming them to Blighton Valley, population 8,778. Alyssa started to get nervous. She could feel the sweat on her palms and tried to ignore it as the first residential buildings came into view. They were still on the outskirts of town and could see the occasional cow or horse sleeping in their darkened pastures. Tessa helpfully pointed out everything as they saw it and gave her the word for it in French.

"That's a *chèvre*." She pointed to a goat tethered to a stake outside someone's house. "And that," She pointed to the moon, just visible through the windshield, "is *la lune*."

"What's the word for robber?" Ella wanted to know. Tessa grinned.

"Brigand."

"*Nous sommes brigands*," Rita exclaimed, "or would that change for feminine? Oh well…"

There was a slight chuckling in the van as they came into the main part of town.

"How long until we get there?" Alyssa's teeth were suddenly chattering and the joke about *brigands* didn't seem nearly so funny anymore.

Dawn looked at her watch. "About three minutes. Are you nervous?" Alyssa shrugged in embarrassment.

Dawn reached back awkwardly to pat her arm. "Don't worry, we're good thieves." This did almost nothing to reassure her, but nonetheless, Alyssa attempted a smile and gave herself a mental shake. This was the cost of living away from her dad, of being her own person.

The Salvation Army thrift store appeared on the left side of the road and Ella brought the van into the parking lot. Instead of cutting the engine she kept going, driving another hundred yards or so. She parked on the side of the road and turned off the van.

"Stay close behind me," Dawn instructed in a whisper, and Alyssa nodded as they piled out of the van.

It was a short walk to the store but it stretched longer as Alyssa's nervousness increased, anticipations and reservations seeking mind space as she walked. They did not approach the door directly, but instead went around to the left and hugged the wall, inching steadily along. The closest streetlight was at the end of the parking lot behind a low hanging maple. Dawn checked their surroundings, cautiously and meticulously scanning for the slightest details. There was nothing and she nodded, giving the signal for advance.

Ella went down on one knee and Tessa behind her climbed onto her shoulders, holding one of the small black pouches Rita had shown Alyssa in the van. Ella stood up carefully and the group crept forward, following their stacked comrades to a few feet behind the door. Quickly and carefully Tessa reached up, putting her arm over the security camera that protruded from the door and deftly hooking the pouch over the lens.

Ella knelt down again. Tessa climbed off so Ella could begin to pick the lock. It didn't take nearly as long as Alyssa had expected. Her heart was pounding, reminding her that every second they might be spotted. *Click*, the lock gave and Ella pushed the door open. The Barn Brigade moved into the storage room of the Salvation Army and spread out, just as they had on the fateful trip to the Redfield supermarket.

The coast was clear. Deserted. The girls followed Dawn into the main part of the store. They didn't waste time looking for anything stylish or fancy, at least not for Alyssa. Her burglar bag soon bulged with shirts bearing the mottos of bands she'd never listened to and movies she'd never seen. Rita also picked up a few more spoons and forks from the kitchen section. Ella meanwhile was pushing hurriedly through a rack of jeans, trying to find something to go with her top. She was finding little but more of what they already had: worn out pants with more holes than a sponge. Tessa slipped away for a moment and returned with a forest green scarf for Ella to wear to the interview. Dawn silently nodded her consent and went on running her hands over the denim. Rita, flipping through a rack at the other end of the large section, waved Alyssa over. The younger girl grinned when she saw what Rita was holding and jabbed a thumb at the others.

Ella did raise her eyebrows when she saw the skirt, but at least she didn't raise an objection. The Barn Brigade did one more quick circuit of the store, searching for anything else they might need. Dawn picked up a winter hat and added it to her already bulging bag.

They left the store without incident, but after the door was relocked and Tessa was up on Ella's shoulders to remove the camera blind, something went wrong. As Tessa's hand extended, fingers reaching for the bag, a fox, just a small red one, darted past the group and disappeared behind the dumpster. The sudden movement was just enough to make Ella look around, and that small shift was just enough to make Tessa lose her grip. Her hand shot into the camera's range just as the bag fluttered to the ground beyond their reach. She floundered, trying to pull back behind the camera without exposing any more of herself. Tessa's hands landed on the ridged braids on top of Ella's head and the older girl backed up quickly, setting Tessa down and leading the flight for the van.

The Barn Brigade was shaken when Ella finally started the engine and pulled out of there. It was a potentially fatal mistake. If the store workers saw that clip of Tessa's hand dropping the bag, or found the bag itself and called the police, they knew they were in trouble. They were quiet for a long time on the drive home. Even though they'd gotten what they'd come for, this slip-up was just a bit too close for comfort. It was not until the unlit and slightly forbidding yet utterly beautiful shape of the barn rose to the left of the road that Alyssa dared to break the silence.

"Well, at least we can start our plan tomorrow." She tried to sound upbeat but the potential setback was still jangling her nerves and her leg kept twitching as the adrenaline worked through her, slowly releasing its hold on her nervous system.

Rita jumped out and ran to the door, opening it with the key around her neck and standing off to the side as Ella drove the others in. As soon as the door was safely barricaded and the Barn Brigade returned to the basement they began unloading their loot.

"There's no use trying to sleep right after a raid," Ella told Alyssa as they upended the bags they'd filled in the Salvation Army. "You've still got way too much energy." Rita nodded and dumped out her own sack right next to theirs. The effect was rather like that of small children comparing their hauls of Halloween candy and the thought made Alyssa sad. She'd been in the hospital on Halloween. Unconsciously she ran a finger over the smooth texturing of her scarred cheek, a certain melancholy momentarily overcoming her.

"Wow, this is quite something!" Ella held up her outfit, the black shirt they'd found earlier with the green scarf around the neck. On her lap rested the skirt, a calf length loose fitting black peasant skirt. It was really quite a nice combination. Ella glanced over at the ladder, at whose base were aligned six pairs of shoes. Hers, being the largest, resided at the end, a dubious grayish white in color. Dawn saw her looking.

"It doesn't matter. They're not going to decide not to take you on as an intern just because your shoes don't match." She turned back to her own pile of clothes and pulled out the hat. It was red with gray stripes and braided tassels to tie under the chin. She put it on.

"Very classy!" Rita told her and Dawn grinned.

"I haven't got a winter hat. Of course, it's a bit late for that now, but at least I'll have it next year." Tessa nodded and stood up to bring the basket out from behind the curtain. Everyone took turns folding clothes and placing them neatly into the basket. When they were done it was piled at least a foot and a half above the top edge. Rita had to be very careful when she pushed it back where it went. The other stolen items were distributed accordingly: cutlery was washed thoroughly and put away in the mugs that held them and the new cushion Tessa had picked up was stowed beneath the table.

"I don't know about you all, but I'm going to bed," Ella said at last, stretching her mouth in an enormous yawn.

Dawn agreed and the usual bedtime routine was followed for the second time that night.

"I think we should take a shower tomorrow," Tessa announced as she emerged from the curtain clad in her pajamas. Alyssa had been wondering how they were going to take showers here. She'd seen swimming suits hanging on the inside of the curtain rail and the one Dawn had selected for her — plain navy with electric green straps — but she hadn't really questioned their use until now.

"How do you guys shower?" she asked, and Rita pointed to the bar of soap lying dormant on the shelf.

"We take that down to the creek twice a week and scrub ourselves silly."

"What about shampoo?"

"If you don't use shampoo for a while your hair starts doing what it's supposed to, as long as you get it wet from time to time, which is basically distributing oils everywhere and looking like Dawn's."

Alyssa looked at Dawn's short brown hair. It looked pretty normal, so she just shrugged and took her turn behind the curtain.

27

Liz scrolled absently through the chain of security shots. They were labeled by the hour and played in fast forward, in case anyone had done something suspicious, which was unlikely around here. Anyone desperate enough to come to the Salvation Army probably didn't have much cash, but no one robbed a charity, for goodness sake. The only reason she even watched the little three-minute clips was because it was her job and she didn't want a reputation for being a slacker.

Suddenly the screen went black. Liz frowned and thumped on the console a few times. Honestly, these worn-out old machines, this happened every once in a while. But even as quickly, the image returned and Liz could clearly see a hand reach forward and drop something. It happened so fast she was almost convinced she'd imagined it, but just in case she slowed the tape down and took another look.

No doubt about it. A hand with dirty fingernails, holding a scrap of...something. Whatever it was fluttered to the ground as the hand dropped out of sight. Liz backed up the tape again, to the place where it had gone black. She watched it at normal speed. Sure enough, it hadn't been a system error; Liz could see now, the arc of blackness being snatched over the screen. Someone had blinded the camera.

She paused the tape and stood up, stretching as she moved to the back door of the Salvation Army. Opening it, she looked down and saw what she knew she would: A small black pouch made of the fabric used for theater curtains. Liz cursed.

28

Even though they'd been up half the night, the Barn Brigade rose promptly at seven the next morning and had breakfast in their pajamas. After eating a small serving each of instant oatmeal, the girls split into their work teams. Instead of cleaning the Barn, Rita and Dawn's reduced group took turns changing into their swimming suits while Alyssa, Ella, and Tessa washed the dishes. They switched halfway through and Alyssa was pleased to discover that her swimsuit was only a little too big.

It was relatively warm in the Barn, but as soon as the girls got outside, legs sprouted goose bumps.

"It's freezing!" Alyssa exclaimed and Dawn agreed. "Let's run!"

Alyssa herself was not big on that idea, but followed obediently as her new friends took off at a swift jog towards the small wood behind the Barn. It was a good fifteen-minute run and Alyssa felt her throat go dry and cold before they arrived. The water was not in the least inviting; it was iron gray and very shallow. Alyssa shivered as she took off a shoe to dip in her toe. Dawn on the other hand plunged straight in, kneeling on the rocky bed in her deep red swimsuit and splashing water over her arms. Tessa followed her, shivering as she gingerly moved closer to the center of the creek. Alyssa was not so careful when she finally worked up the nerve to enter. There was a thin covering of algae over many rocks on the bottom of the creek. It was rather slippery and Alyssa found herself stepping wrong as soon as she'd entered. She fell down hard on her back in the icy water.

"Ouch!"

"Are you all right?" Rita waded in to stand over her. Rita's comically purple bikini was the only two-piece in the group and it dwarfed her pale blue eyes to an alarming extent.

"Yup, I'm fine. Just a little…cold." Rita laughed and sat down slowly beside her, careful not to splash.

"You ever bathed in a creek before?"

Alyssa shook her head. "Is it that different from bathing in a bath tub?"

"Immensely." Rita grinned and clapped her hands, they made lower, almost hollow sound with the water dripping off them. Ella heard the noise and took careful aim with the soap, tossing it to her energetic companion as she swiftly joined them in the creek.

Rita wet the soap and rubbed it between her hands, getting a fair amount of the yellow substance between her fingers.

"Here." Rita tossed the soap to Alyssa and began rubbing her own arms. Alyssa had to dive to catch the slippery object and ended up landing on her elbow, with her face just barely above the water, the soap clutched in her free arm. She imitated what Rita had done and passed the bar to Dawn.

"You've got to get a little bit of sand into the soap too," Ella told her as she reached to the bank for some, "it's good for your skin."

Though she may have been right, Alyssa still didn't exactly want to rub herself with river gunk. She did as she was told, however, and soon found it to be quite a painful experience.

"How do you stand that?" Alyssa asked Tessa, who now had the soap and was passing it to Ella, upstream from them. The older girl shrugged.

"I guess I've just gotten used to it. You will too — don't worry." Alyssa rinsed her arms and shook them off; the backs were red from the sand scrubbing and stung slightly in the cold water.

"Now dunk your head." Dawn instructed.

"What?" I don't want to do that! This water's seriously cold!"

"Exactly!" Dawn plugged her nose and immersed herself completely in the steely creek. Alyssa winced. Rita grinned wickedly at the newcomer and, favoring a voluntary dunking over a forced one, Alyssa closed her eyes and thrust her head beneath the surface. The water seemed to press against her eyeballs, freezing them inside her head. She shook out her hair and ran her fingers through the recently cropped strands. Now she was glad Dawn had cut it; bathing here without conditioner would have been a nightmare.

Alyssa came up for air, gasping from the vicious chill of the morning. It almost felt good. Her skin stung in the breeze. Now fully wet, she shivered anew in its harsh gust. Dawn, upstream, waved for the rest of them to clear the path. Perplexed, Alyssa paddled farther into the center of the creek and swam slowly upstream to stay still. Dawn lay down in the water and floated on her back down the current. Her short brown hair floated outwards from her head, drifting idly as Dawn enjoyed the slow, gentle motion of the stream.

"My turn!" Tessa went after Dawn, paddling slightly to keep afloat.

"Can I try?" Alyssa suddenly felt timid, but at Ella's nod of consent traversed her way to where the others were waiting. She lay down in the water and tried to relax, taking in a huge breath and letting her bottom rise off the creek bed. It was fun. She hadn't been swimming for quite a while and it felt nice to let the current carry her.

"Oi!" Ella called from up the bank, "Look out!" Alyssa yanked her head up in time to see that she was headed straight towards a rotting log.

"Oh no!" She hit it with her foot and the wood gave, squishing like a sponge under her bare toes.

'Eew! Gross, it's squishy!" She found the bottom of the creek with her toes and backpedaled straight into Rita as she came floating towards her. They collided with a large splash. Both their heads went under for a moment and then they were up, tangled together in a mess of flailing arms and laughter.

"Aren't you going to go?" Alyssa asked Ella as soon as she was finally free of Rita's limbs.

"I can't, if I do my hair will get all frizzy, and that's the last thing I need right now."

"Fair enough." Alyssa stepped onto the bank and shook out her hair, getting everyone slightly wetter in the process, then leaned down to put on her shoes.

"Why didn't you bring a towel?" she asked Dawn, who had followed her out of the creek.

"We don't need one. We'll be dry by the time we get back anyway — all but our hair."

"What do you do in the winter?" That was another thing Alyssa had been wondering.

"We boil a ton of water, lug it up to the gym and take turns sponging ourselves down and rinsing out our hair. It's actually easier than coming here because everyone gets to go on their own, more privacy. The barn gets pretty cold though, so that's tough."

"You bathe in boiling water?"

Dawn raised an amused eyebrow. "No, it gets cold really fast. That's just how we make sure it doesn't give us hypothermia."

"Ah."

The other Brigadiers were getting out of the creek, shivering as the cold air hit them.

"Let's go, I'm freezing!" Rita ran a rand through her hair and bent down beside Tessa to tie her shoes.

Dawn nodded, rubbing her arms absentmindedly as she stared through the sparse wood to where, across the soybean field, they could just see the tip of the barn's roof.

Tessa finished squeezing out her hair and they were off. This time it felt good to Alyssa to run. The wind was still on her, sending the droplets that clung to her flying out behind, but her swiftly beating heart warmed the skin they clung to. By the time they returned to the barn, Alyssa was out of breath, but warm and nearly dry.

There was a single towel behind the curtain, apart from the curtain itself, but otherwise no way of getting dry. Alyssa hung her bathing suit up on the curtain rail and got dressed. She put on one of her new outfits, a pair of worn jeans and a long-sleeved purple shirt, and stepped out from behind the curtain. Dawn took her place and Alyssa went to the shelf where sat, neatly arranged, an assortment of hairbrushes and combs. Ella with her cornrow braids hardly ever used hers, and so over the past few days Alyssa had adopted them. Her new haircut was a thousand times easier to handle and she liked the way it turned in at her chin. She brushed her hair until she couldn't find any tangles, then put on a headband and sat down on her bed.

It had been decided that only Ella and Dawn would be going to the internship interview. It was too risky to bring Alyssa in broad daylight and there was a slight possibility that the authorities knew about Tessa too, now that Sabrina was caught. Rita hadn't really cared either way, but had opted not to endure the boring drive into Redfield or the trip to the library where Ella would use the public computer to forge herself a resume and application.

Ella looked great in her black clothes and green scarf, and although the shoes were still all wrong, they weren't all that noticeable. Tessa stared critically at her friend, looking her over from top to bottom.

"You look great.," she decided. Ella pretended to slap her.

"You're just saying that. I always look like this."

"Exactly!" Tessa looked overtly mischievous.

Ella just rolled her eyes, looking deservedly abashed, but also a bit pleased.

29

Ben Windham was not accustomed to doing any sort of hard work. His job was basically to sit around all day and make sure none of the children in the Social Services Center orphanage decided to wander out. He also directed volunteers to the kitchen, but that was pretty much it. Sure, he'd had a few odd jobs from time to time: his higher-ups would drop by and tell him to clean the fish tank, or one of the aides would ask if he could go get more of something or other, but nothing really unusual or unpleasant. Then today this young woman just walked in and applied for an unoffered internship.

"Excuse me, sir?" Ben looked up. The woman he was looking at smiled shyly.

"How can I help you?" he grunted, sitting up straighter.

"I'm wondering if you have any intern openings right now." Ben looked at the sign-in sheet on the desk beside him. There seemed to be several openings. The numbers went up to thirty but the employee names stopped at eighteen. An intern could help fill the gap.

"What are your qualifications?" Ben thought he might as well do it right.

"I'm certified in first aid and I am currently taking a semester break from Prudence Redfield University where I'm studying engineering."

"Is that all?"

The woman shuffled her feet, but pulled a folder from her bag. "Here's my background. All my previous jobs, schools, and accomplishments are listed along with an official request for an internship with references from my school." She placed the folder on Ben's desk and stepped back, clasping her hands on her skirt expectantly.

Ben took a few minutes to skim her information. There was a section for 'criminal record' on the application, but there was nothing in it. After flipping through the page of previous jobs, most of which were the typical sort of part-time things you expect from teenagers, and briefly glancing over the signatures from former managers and teachers, he made his decision.

"OK, I don't see why not."

The woman blinked at him. "Really? Thank you so much! This will be so great when I apply for a serious job. Thanks! When is the best time for me to help out?"

Ben looked down at the list of shifts and stroked his thin mustache. "Er, how about you come tomorrow evening and get acquainted with everyone. Get here about six o'clock to fill out forms and start your shift. Will Fridays, Sundays, and Mondays be all right? How many hours do you need?"

"I'm sure that will be fine, but I need you to sign this sheet." She indicated a piece of paper towards the back of the folder. Ben did as he was told and signed with a flourish. Ella smiled happily.

"Thank you. I'll see you tomorrow at six then." She turned and left. Ben wasn't quite sure if he was allowed to hire people, but she seemed nice enough, he supposed she'd do a decent job. He watched her get into an old green van across the street and start the engine. Ben shrugged. He put his head down on his desk and closed his eyes. All this commotion lately with that missing girl Alyssa what's-her-name and cops rushing in and out asking about that other new girl... Ben needed a nap.

30

Alyssa still couldn't believe the Barn Brigadiers did whatever Dawn told them to. Even having felt the effect herself, and finally understanding Dawn's well-kept secret, she didn't know why they had to exercise without her.

"But we just got clean." She turned over on her bed to face the wall and squeezed her eyes shut. Her hair wasn't even dry yet. "I don't want to get all sweaty again."

"We can do something fun today," Tessa coaxed.

"Like what?"

The older girl hesitated. "Like gymnastics, or yoga, or… or… self defense."

Alyssa turned over again and opened one eye, like a reluctant child being woken up for school. "Do you know all those?"

Tessa shrugged. "Well enough to fake them. Come on!"

Alyssa let her arm flop off the mattress, then a leg. Then she heaved herself up and followed Tessa out of the basement.

"Where's Rita?" Alyssa asked, noticing the exuberant blonde's absence.

"Upstairs. What do you want to do today?"

"Of those choices? Gymnastics."

"OK. We'll do some partner and trio work."

Alyssa yawned, but obediently climbed the ladder to the gym.

Rita was in the middle of the room lying on her back, arms splayed and eyes closed. Alyssa tried to give Tessa a here-is-my-point kind of look, but couldn't because Tessa was no longer behind her.

"Wake up!" Tessa poked Rita's arm.

"I'm awake." Rita didn't sound very sure.

"OK, then get up. How come you're all so tired all of a sudden?"

Alyssa snickered at that one. "If you think about it," she pointed out innocently, "we only got like, five hours of sleep last night."

Tessa seemed to have forgotten, but she tugged on Rita's arm and brought her to her knees anyway.

"We can stretch first, if you want."

"Can we do lazy man yoga?" Rita asked hopefully. Tessa rolled her eyes.

"What's lazy man yoga?" Alyssa knelt beside them and Rita's eyes shot open.

"Pure bliss." Rita replied fervently. Tessa rolled her eyes again.

"OK, now you have to show me," Alyssa said.

"I don't actually know how to do it, I just make it up as I go along. And it's called Thai yoga, not lazy man yoga."

"That's OK, just let Alyssa see, you can demonstrate on me." Tessa snorted but took hold of Rita's leg and bent it at the knee, placing her other hand on Rita's outstretched leg and pressing them apart in a gentle stretch. After a few seconds she slowly switched the legs' positions and leaned into the stretch as if they were her muscles being loosened, not Rita's.

Next she moved around to sit behind the older girl's shoulder and reached for her leg. She moved it around in its hip socket and pulled it gently towards Rita's face. They went on like this, Tessa moving Rita's limbs around and Rita staying as still as she could for about five minutes before Tessa set down the final elbow and turned to Alyssa.

"Your turn."

It was a very strange feeling, and Alyssa found herself wanting to move on her own to help Tessa, but she just kept still, relaxing as her limbs were pulled and pushed and her muscles woke up for the second time that day.

"Wow!" she said when it was over and Tessa had stepped away. "That was really cool!" Rita nodded and Tessa looked slightly pleased with herself.

"Anyway, time for exercises!" Rita jumped to her feet, in mock enthusiasm, "Horrah!"

Alyssa cocked her head at her, and Rita's shoulders slumped.

"Who am I kidding? I'm not at all excited for this." Rita admitted.

Tessa led them through another round of stretches, self-mobilized this time, and then proceeded to help Rita teach Alyssa the basics of partner gymnastics.

After an hour and a half of instruction, Alyssa had stood on Rita's shoulders, done double and triple somersaults, been lifted and twirled on Tessa's feet, and launched across the room in an assisted back flip. Panting and sweaty, she flopped down on the ground, staring blandly into the hole where the shingle was missing.

"Hey, don't give up now, we've still got to do conditioning!" Alyssa propped herself up on one elbow.

"What's that?"

"Calisthenics."

"What's *that?*"

Tessa shook her head in amused exasperation. "You know, sit-ups and leg lifts and arm circles and such."

Alyssa did not attempt to conceal her displeasure. "Oh, joy."

"Or I suppose you could just climb the rope again..." Tessa looked away guiltily as she offered the simpler option.

Alyssa jumped up and rushed to the climbing rope. Tessa snickered.

"I had a feeling you'd choose that option. Climb up and touch the roof."

Alyssa's arms had never recovered from the first workout she'd been made to endure at the Barn, but she could actually see the growing bulge of her muscles. Today she managed to reach the ceiling — partly because she hadn't just spent an hour swinging around hand weights, and partly because she'd gotten a little more accustomed to it. Nevertheless, her arms burned by the time she was on the ground again.

"My turn!" Tessa grabbed the rope and swung herself up it easily, touching the knot at the top. She returned to the ground, but instead of touching down, she dangled at the bottom and wrapped her other leg.

"No way!" Alyssa was duly impressed as the older girl made her way— a bit slower this time— to the ceiling. Tessa leaped gratefully to the ground a few seconds later and pointed accusingly at Rita, who was sneaking stealthily towards the ladder.

"Oh, no you don't! Do French climbs all the way to the top!" Rita turned around and attempted to assuage Tessa with a clumsy puppy-eyes expression. Tessa grinned but didn't let up. Alyssa watched with mild amusement and moderate interest as Rita created a step for herself by cutting slack between the main rope and her right foot. She placed her left foot in the slack and applied pressure on both sides, putting her weight onto it to find another handhold. When she came down again, Alyssa could see the pink rope impressions left on her feet. She winced. That looked especially painful.

The three of them descended once again into the basement and prepared for tutorial.

"I guess it's French again?" Alyssa cocked her head as Tessa went to the whiteboard.

"Yes, unless you have something you want to teach." Alyssa didn't, so they went ahead with the lesson. Rita, it was decided, could mind her own business while Tessa did her best to catch the newcomer up.

"*Je m'appelle Thérèse.*" She pointed at herself. "*Comment t'appeles-tu?*" She pointed at Alyssa.

"*Je m'appelle...*" She broke off, switching to English, "My name?"

Tessa nodded.

"*Je m'appelle* Alyssa."

Rita snorted loudly from across the room and Alyssa made a face at her.

"You need a more French sounding name." Tessa told her, "I'm Thérèse, like Teresa? It sounds better in French. Anyway, you should probably be Elise."

"OK. How do you say 'my name is' again?"

31

"We're back!"

Ella looked exhausted; so did Dawn, for that matter. The leader didn't even bother to say hello. She just staggered across the room and flopped onto her cot.

"She sure is sleeping a lot lately," Rita observed, and Ella gave her a sharp look.

"She has a right to, especially now, because the next few days are going to be even rougher than the last few. I'll be happy to get some rest myself if this mess is ever over."

"I heard that!" Dawn lifted her head. "You mean when it's over. I'm not tolerating any pessimism here. We're getting Sabrina back no matter what." With that she pulled her sleeping bag over her face and said no more.

"What time is it anyway?" Ella looked at her watch. "I'm hungry!"

"Why? what time is it?" Tessa acted as if this was somehow urgent.

"Four thirty."

"Then, how about Alyssa, Rita and I start a nice dinner and you read aloud to us."

"So glad to be of service," Alyssa muttered, but no one heard her, and Rita beat everyone to the bookcase to choose a book.

"How about…this one?" She pulled a book off the shelf. It looked kind of old, with a scuffed black cover. Rita looked extra pleased with herself as she stuck the volume under Ella's nose.

"Winnie the Pooh?"

The blonde nodded shyly and Ella shrugged, opening the book to the first page.

"'Here is Edward Bear, coming downstairs now, bump, bump, bump, on the back of his head behind Christopher Robin.'" Ella read well, and although she didn't give the characters voices or anything, the others nonetheless felt deeply engaged with the book as they sat, checking the boiling pasta from time to time, and generally enjoying the sound of Ella's voice. By the time dinner was ready they'd already read three stories and Dawn was awake and listening. Rita reached into the pot with a pair of tongs and removed what looked like a tin can.

"What the heck is that?" Ella said, putting down the book to stare.

"The tomato sauce."

"Why on earth is it in the pasta?" Rita set it down on the tabletop and gripped it with a dishrag over her hand, brandishing a can opener with the other. "To warm it up. I didn't want to have to use another pan. Now keep going — you're almost at the end of that chapter."

"Hold it!" Dawn was out of her bed and next to Rita before the latter could puncture the can. "If you open it while it's that hot it'll spray everywhere."

"Really?" Rita sounded as if she wanted to try it.

"Really. Now just put it in tepid water for a minute and we'll let it sit while we serve ourselves. It should be safe to open by then." The leader didn't sound too sure about that last part. All the same, she bounced to her place with uncharacteristic vigor. "I'm hungry!"

"You're energetic, too," Alyssa commented and she was greeted by a very unexpected grin.

"Yes I am!" Dawn shoveled pasta onto her plate. The others watched in a mild state of shock as Dawn consumed her noodles.

"I thought you were exhausted." Alyssa put her head on one side.

"I was, but I love noodles and I've just had an idea."

"Oh, what's that then?" asked Alyssa.

Dawn paused for dramatic affect, something no one had ever seen her do before.

"Well, you know that one enormous gap in our plan? I've figured it out."

"Oh, how?" Ella was skeptical, as were the rest of them.

Dawn crooked a finger under her chin, turning to look pointedly at an unnerved Tessa. "How averse is Sabrina to pain?"

That was not what Tessa had been expecting at all. "Why do you need to know, 'cause I'm not going to let you cut up my sister, or burn her or get her in a car crash just so it looks like she died."

Dawn smirked. "Don't worry. She'll be fine in the long run."

Tessa didn't look especially satisfied with that, but said no more in objection. "She can take a lot, I guess. Pain-wise, I mean."

"Good, that's settled then."

"OK," Ella decided, "I'm officially scared of you."

32

"Dawn, could you explain exactly how I'm supposed to give this to her again?" Ella held up an envelope she'd just sealed and waved it around.

"Did you include everything I told you to?"

"I did."

"Good, then you'll just carry that around with you while you work until you find a way to slip it to her."

"I was afraid you'd say something like that."

Dawn frowned. "What is that supposed to mean?"

"It means that there's a lot that could go wrong with this little plan of yours and I just don't want to be the one to mess it up," Ella admitted. A few days ago, Dawn would have been enraged at this comment and it still tweaked her fuse a little bit, but not enough to set it aflame.

"I know that, but there's nothing I can do, so please try?" Ella saw the desperation and annoyance on Dawn's face and just nodded.

It was getting late and Alyssa tried hard to stifle a yawn as Ella finished packing her bag for the next day. Still, she didn't feel ready to go to bed, leaving the others to fret about the day to come.

"I'm going to get in my pajamas," Alyssa said at last. "Don't come back here, all right?" At the universal nod of acknowledgement, Alyssa slipped behind the curtain. She put on the baggy T-shirt and sweat pants that she had designated as pajamas from last night's haul. They were comfortable, but nothing special. She stepped out from behind the curtain. No one had moved. She brushed her hair and teeth in silence and climbed onto her bed.

"You're sleeping already?" Rita looked rather confused.

"No," Alyssa blushed a little, "I just don't have anything better to do. In fact, I was kind of hoping that Ella would read for a while." Alyssa looked hopefully at Ella who smiled.

"That sounds great. I like reading to you guys." She retrieved the Winnie the Pooh book from where she'd left it on the whiteboard stand and opened it to the beginning of the fourth story. Alyssa fell asleep after a few stories, but the others stayed awake, Dawn organizing the bookcase to relieve her stress, and Rita rubbing Ella's feet as she read. It would have been peaceful, but for the sight of Tessa, huddled by the bookshelf. Though the twins were not the smug inseparable type it was still odd to see one without knowing the other was nearby.

Rita felt a sudden compassion for Tessa, all alone here and an even deeper, more unexpected one for Sabrina even more alone somewhere else. She shook her head; after tomorrow they'd be together. The entire Barn Brigade as one. She refused to let some of her thoughts surface, thoughts concerning Sabrina's motives for departure, her feelings towards those motives, Tessa's sister, and Dawn. Would Sabrina want to come back? Would she willingly go along with the plan they had concocted or would she scorn it in favor of a newfound community? Rita closed her eyes and let the serenity of Ella's voice telling carefree stories drive all notions of uncertainty from her mind.

33

Sabrina had grown accustomed to the sounds of breathing at night; to falling asleep among the peaceful exhales of the Barn Brigade. She'd always thought it nice that she could know where everyone was and whether they were asleep without even opening her eyes. She didn't have that here. Leann snored through her nose and the sound of the wind through the open window was alien to her. Sabrina hadn't slept in a room with a window in months. She turned over.

It had definitely been a mistake to run away from the barn. Maybe if she hadn't been caught she'd have gone back by now. It was a bitter thought. She turned over and plugged her ears, trying not to think about Tessa. Her sister had always relied on her. It had been an idiotic thing to do, leaving her alone. Sabrina immediately felt guilty for thinking of it like that. *She's not alone, she has Rita and Ella and...and the others. You're alone though; all you have is Gabby the poodle.* Sabrina frowned. It wasn't nice to refer to her like that.

She closed her eyes. *I wish you were here, Tess. I love you.* Just thinking it didn't feel like enough, so Sabrina put her finger to the wall, and eyes still closed, traced the words over the blobby white paint. She fell asleep with reluctant tears in her eyes.

34

Around eleven o'clock Dawn slid the last book into place and stepped back to admire her work.

Ella sighed and closed the book at the end of the next story. "I'm tired."

"Yeah, me too." Dawn took the book from her friend and stowed it on the shelf in the place she'd left for it.

Rita was already asleep with her head on the table. Ella prodded her. Once all were in bed and the lights were out, only Tessa stayed awake. She stared into the utter darkness to where she knew Alyssa lay asleep. She could hear her subtle breathing, a faint hiss. To her left, where Sabrina should be, the familiar sound of her sister's nocturnal sighs was missing. The two of them had shared a room their whole life. Tessa couldn't remember the last time she'd been without her sister for more than a day. She bit her lip and squeezed her eyes shut. *Don't worry, Sabrina, we'll get you back. I love you.* In the darkness with her head under the sleeping bag, Tessa could almost believe Sabrina was right nearby.

The next morning Rita and Alyssa decided it would be nice to have a picnic breakfast. Though Dawn was not too keen on the risk, she finally gave in and even helped the others to move the breakfast stuff outside. They put down a cloth in the middle of the CTM field and returned for water, cups, silverware, and finally, the food. They were having real oatmeal. It was rare that they didn't use the instant variety but Alyssa had unearthed it and they couldn't find an expiration date on the package, so that was that. It smelled wonderful as Tessa stirred the pot lovingly with a plastic spoon.

"Do we have any brown sugar for it?" Alyssa hadn't seen any and Tessa shook her head. "We do have honey though, if you like that." Tessa held out the small bear-shaped bottle.

Even Dawn enjoyed the peaceful meal on the dying quack grass in the soybean field. Alyssa took the opportunity to ask yet another question that had wormed its way into her mind while rummaging around in the food cupboard that morning.

"Are you all vegetarians or something? There's not a single meat dish in the entire cupboard." Dawn grinned.

"There's a reason for that." Dawn said, a bit more sharply than had become usual in the last few days.

"And what is it?" Alyssa cocked her head on one side.

"Well, a lot of meat is perishable, so that's one reason and the other is because, even if it comes in a can, being just a tiny bit undercooked it can make you sick."

"But that hardly ever happens, right?" Alyssa wasn't too sure.

"You're right," Dawn admitted, "but it's way too inconvenient to risk it happening around here."

Alyssa shrugged. "To be honest I don't really care too much."

"That's settled then." Dawn turned to Rita. "Can you pass the honey?" The other girl obliged and Dawn put some on her oatmeal.

It took a lot longer to clear everything into the barn than it had to bring it out. Somehow they couldn't quite carry it all at once, but finally they managed to bring in the picnic blanket and settle into their morning routine. Once they were all back in the basement Ella brought out the Pooh book again, and the others set to work on the dishes.

It was relatively quiet in the Barn for almost half an hour but for the subtle clanking of soapy bowls and the soft murmur of Ella's voice.

At last, when all the dishes were done, the satisfied group moved up to the gym where they spent the next half hour doing what passed for karate under Rita's instruction. They left out the shouting part, to Alyssa's disappointment, but were nevertheless tired out by the time Rita had them get on the floor for conditioning. The day before, Alyssa had seen Rita's abdominal muscles when she'd worn her bathing suit. She was strong for a reason, and the reason was, Alyssa soon discovered, that she loved core workouts. Hundreds of sit-ups, plank holds and leg-lifts later, Alyssa was afraid to laugh for fear she'd rip her stomach muscles. She climbed down the ladder very gingerly and plopped down on a cushion for tutorial. Dawn grabbed her beneath the armpits and playfully hauled her up again.

"You're teaching today."

Alyssa was taken aback. "What? Why?"

"Because you haven't done it yet and it's about time." In her mind, Alyssa thought resentfully that Dawn seemed to have reverted to her pre-confession state of mind, but she went to the whiteboard nonetheless.

"But what can I teach you? You're all older than me."

"That's true, but I'm sure you know something we don't."

"Wanna bet?" Alyssa wracked her brain for something she could pull out for these girls. "It can be anything?" She inquired at last.

Dawn nodded encouragingly.

"It doesn't have to be an academic subject," Rita cut in, and Dawn looked at her suspiciously. "You don't want it to be academic, do you?" Rita finished.

"I have an idea." Alyssa was kind of embarrassed but said it anyway. "I'm going to teach you a song. Like in choir, you know?"

"Yay!" Rita looked way too excited. "What kind of a song?"

"A blessing song. It's got two short parts."

"How would you like us to split?" Ella was obviously trying to help her out.

"You can just stay like that for now. I'm going to teach all of you both parts so you can switch every time you start over. The words for the first part go like this: *In sunlight and moonlight, under the sky, may you always be jovial, carefree and spry. Through winter and spring, summer and fall, may your people be prosperous, your troubles be small.*"

The others repeated, letting the words rest and settle in their mouths.

"Here." Alyssa picked up a marker. "I'll write the words on the board." When she was done she turned back to her friends.

"I guess I'll sing it now." A slight blush crept onto her cheekbones, coloring her pale scar a bright pink. The melody was sweet. It moved up and down in pretty little steps but it was also a bit sad. When she was done, Alyssa had the rest of the Barn Brigade repeat each line after her. They were no opera group, but their voices weren't half bad.

"OK. Do you think we can try that all together now?" Alyssa still felt a bit timid but she counted out four beats and sang along with the rest of them.

"Great!" She turned to the whiteboard and wrote the second part below the first.

"This one has a different melody." She sang it for them. "*May fortune match your beauty and riches match your health, may your good luck outweigh you in laughter and wealth.*"

"That one's even prettier!" Rita exclaimed, and sang happily line by line as Alyssa repeated the part.

"That was good. Let's try it together once." She counted out the beat and the Barn Brigade sang the second, higher part.

"All right. Let's just alternate the parts for a while until you've got them memorized." She conducted them through. The first part slid into the second wonderfully and it slid back with a melodious pick up. After three times through Alyssa stopped them.

"That sounds amazing. Are you ready to try it together?" There was a general nod of agreement. So Alyssa went on. "OK, what we're going to do is have Rita and Ella sing this part first." She pointed to the first part she'd written on the board. "Dawn and Tess will sing the other one. After one time through you switch to the other part. Do you understand?"

"Yup!" Rita was still looking far too excited, but the others gave an affirmative as well, so Alyssa gave each group their notes and counted them in. The harmony was wonderful and although the rhythm slipped around a little it still made the barn seem too small a place for such a nice sound.

"Wow!" Ella exclaimed after they were done, "That was fun. I didn't know all of you could sing so well." Alyssa grinned, a bit embarrassed, but happy.

"That's going to be stuck in my head for a while." Dawn smiled as she said it, as if she didn't even care. "Anyway, after lunch we should all take a nap. We're going to be up all night again."

"That sounds great. What's for lunch?" Rita looked hungrily at the chemistry table.

Tessa opened the cupboard. "Macaroni and cheese?" No one particularly cared so Tessa took out the box and started to boil some water.

"I wish it was still summer." Ella turned to Alyssa. "We have this little vegetable garden so we don't have to go steal stuff as often. Plus fresh food is amazing after eating that stuff all year." She shot a contemptuous look at the macaroni box.

"Hey!" Tessa made a pouty face and waved her plastic spoon in the air. Ella sighed wistfully in response.

35

Sabrina stood in what seemed to be an endless line and sighed. Even though volunteers came in to make their food for dinner every day, breakfast was always cereal. Sabrina craned her neck to see the options. Cornflakes, Cheerios, granola, raisin bran... She didn't really care. Sabrina hadn't had milk in so long that no matter what she chose, it tasted disgusting with the cheap powdered milk the orphanage offered.

There was a soft tap on her shoulder and Sabrina grabbed at the hand, knowing from experience that Gabby was the culprit.

"Good morning!"

"You already said that this morning."

"I know, but then you went to have a shower and now you're back, so good morning." Sabrina did not see the logic in this, but decided not to question it as she turned back to face the cereal. There was another tap on her shoulder.

"What do you wanna be when you grow up?" The question took Sabrina by surprise. She hadn't thought about that in a long time. She'd always just assumed she was living towards a certain doom of discovery and punishment, and a prison sentence, or being returned to her parents. She had no hopes for the future, only dread and fear. Quickly she arranged her thoughts and turned the question back to Gabby. "What about you?"

"I want to be a detective!"

Sabrina tried hard to picture that. Gabby did not seem to be the type to wear a trench coat or carry a magnifying glass. Gabby poked Sabrina in the belly.

"YA! Why'd you do that?"

"You were spacing out." She dug her finger in a little harder. By instinct Sabrina flexed her abdominal muscles.

"Whoa! You're so strong!"

"Uh, thanks I guess," Sabrina replied, a little surprised at the compliment.

"You're welcome. Now tell me what you're going to be when you grow up."

Sabrina scrabbled for a suitable answer and said the first thing that came into her head.

"A musician."

"Really?" Gabby's eyes lit up. "What instrument do you play?"

"I don't, not yet anyway."

"Aw." The younger girl was obviously disappointed. "I wanted you to play for us."

"Sorry, I can't." Sabrina reached the front of the line and served herself from the giant cereal dispensers. She couldn't face the milk this early in the morning. Sighing heavily, Sabrina found a place to sit and put her head in her hands.

"What's wrong?" Gabby tried to put her head on the table so she could see Sabrina's face. Sabrina grimaced, but raised her head.

"Nothing, I'm fine."

"Of course you're fine — you don't have to go to school. You're so lucky." Gabby looked enviously up at Sabrina, who did her best to suppress a laugh.

"It's only for a few more days, you know. And half of my supposed free time is taken up by the police anyway, so it's not like I'm having fun or anything."

"You're still lucky. You don't have to cram useless stuff into your head all day."

Sabrina shrugged, trying to end the conversation without being totally rude. The truth was that runaways were not allowed to go to school alone for the first few weeks, just to make sure they didn't run away again. They'd told her as much, and the director of the orphanage had decided it was OK for her to miss a few days school while the police finished cross-examining her and the admissions process was completed. It had been ages since Sabrina had attended school, and she wasn't having much fun with Gabby's antics, either. She sighed again and stood up to get more cereal. How was she ever going to get out of here?

36

Dawn's alarm clock rang at three thirty p.m. and she roused the others quickly. Tension polluted the air as Ella got dressed. She hadn't had a job in years and obviously never under such circumstances. There was one messenger bag in the Barn and that was what Ella carried as they made their way to the van. Inside were a notebook, pen, college textbook so she'd look legitimate, and the letter for Sabrina.

Everyone was going. It had been decided the night before. No one wanted to be left behind on a rescue mission. Although it wasn't the safest option, Dawn understood their need for involvement, although she had insisted on trying to cover Alyssa's scar. They didn't have any makeup to work with and the scar was too close to her nose to cover with a scarf so she did her best with a band-aid. It wasn't perfect but that was just a minor flaw in a plan with many flaws.

Rita flung the Barn door wide and held it as Ella backed out. Ella's hands were moist on the steering wheel. She swallowed as Rita climbed in and buckled her seatbelt. Ella glanced at Dawn and their eyes locked. Dawn hesitated, then smiled and sighed uncertainly. Ella tried a smile too, but it felt false on her face so she just turned the car onto the main road and began the long drive into the city.

There was almost no talk on the way to the Social Services Center. Tessa had her eyes closed and Alyssa stared out the window with a serious expression. Ella went over the plan in her head, over and over. The problem was, it wasn't a very well-formed plan. She had no idea if she'd even be able to put it into action tonight.

Dawn smoothed her hair nervously. She didn't tell herself it would be all right. She knew from experience that this was rarely the case, nothing was ever completely fine. Even the fact that it happened meant it would never be all right again. She bit her lip. No one had said anything about Eric or her mother since she'd told them her story. She had the feeling they were afraid of how she'd react if they tried to bring it up. She'd have to tell Sabrina though, and that would hurt. It had been her fault Sabrina left. She owed her that much, but still, she guiltily almost dreaded Sabrina's return.

Alyssa sat with her knees up; just as she had on the night she'd encountered the Barn Brigade. This time though she wasn't crying and she didn't have to sit on anyone's lap in order to fit. There were only five main seats in the van. Once Sabrina came back, someone would have to sit in the tiny fold-up seats in the third row. Alyssa was also worried. If Sabrina had run away from them, wasn't there a possibility she wouldn't want to come back? Alyssa tried not to think about that. She closed her eyes; there was a certain amount of guilt in her silence. Sabrina had been mad at her when she left. Was she still angry? Would she be resentful? Alyssa had to keep forcing the final question down. She knew the answer but she didn't want to admit it. *Would none of this had happened if I'd never come?*

They approached Redfield all too quickly, with no one's thoughts ready to settle quite yet.

"Can we sing?" Rita looked slightly uncertain but the others though it was a good idea.

"We can sing the song Alyssa taught us, to wish Ella good luck." Tessa laid a hand on the back of her friend's neck; all she could reach from the back of the van.

Ella looked down in embarrassment.

"What's the note we start on?" Dawn asked, and Alyssa hummed it.

"This side of the car start on the lower part and we'll sing the harmony, OK?" She counted out four beats and they moved into song. The song gave voice to everything they could not say aloud. They went through it four or five times before Ella pulled up at a public park about a mile from the orphanage. The final noted faded into silence and everyone but Ella began to unbuckle.

"Good luck." Dawn reached across the driver's seat to hug her friend.

"You too." Ella indicated everyone with her pained smile.

"Don't worry, we'll do fine." Tessa looked more certain than she felt.

"I'll try my best," Ella said at last.

The Barn Brigade was not rash enough to let hope overcome their judgment but they did try their best to encourage Ella as they disembarked. Watching her drive away, each one of them was wishing with all her heart for success.

In the park where they'd been dropped was a jungle gym, all small children gone for the day. It was left to shine dully in the pinkish light of the slowly dropping sun. Here the Barn Brigade waited, concealed among the play equipment, silent in their desperate hopes together.

37

The orphanage aide looked Ella over with a shrewd eye. Ella felt herself blush. She didn't know what was going through this woman's mind, but she didn't associate the expression she now wore with friendliness.

"My name's Tori. It's good to meet you." Ella snapped to attention, looking Tori in the eye.

"It's nice to meet you too. I was told I'd be working as a night aide for the younger children?"

"Yes, that's my area too. I'll just show you around and then you can get to work."

Ella had never spent time in the orphanage so she didn't have to pretend to not know where everything was. Tori led her through the kitchen and dining room, casually pointing out bits of everyday procedure to Ella.

"This is the kitchen. It's very low maintenance. Some volunteers cook in the evenings — in fact they should be arriving any time — but otherwise the meals are pretty much cereal and sandwiches." They passed a small lounge where a few young boys sat playing Monopoly at a round table.

"This is the lounge. The children get to hang around here after school hours. Most of them attend one of the public schools nearby." Tori waved to the two boys, "Phillip,

Mark, this is Ella, she's a new intern here. Ella, this is Phillip and Mark. They're in fifth grade." The two boys grunted hello and Ella did her best to smile at them.

Tori led her up a flight of stairs to the first floor where they passed the dazed fellow who'd offered Ella the position the day before.

"I think you met Ben yesterday. He's in charge of the front desk." She gave him a cheery wave and opened a door on the other side of the room.

"Over here is where the younger children stay. You'll be staying in this room right here when you're not helping out." She indicated a small room to their right. "The light is to stay on at all times. And keep the door open too; young children tend to wake up in the middle of the night. Plan on being a bathroom escort."

"OK." Ella scanned the room; there was a pink armchair and a small filtered drinking water dispenser, a desk, and a cabinet.

"In there," Tori pointed to the cabinet, "you'll find pretty much everything you might need. There's Tylenol and band-aids and stuff in case one of them has an earache or a paper cut or something. It's kept locked, so I asked Ben to give us an extra key. Here." She held out a small key on a neon strap, and Ella obligingly looped it around her neck.

Next they went down the hall to a small playroom where six or seven kids between the ages of three and eight gamboled around.

"See those two doors?" Tori pointed across the playroom. "Those are the dormitories. Left is girls, and right is boys. We have smaller rooms for the older kids but down here everyone's in together."

She turned an abrupt corner and led the way up another flight of stairs.

"Up here is where the older children go. Over here is the supply closet." She pointed to a padlocked door labeled 'Office' and Ella smirked. "The key is kept in that cupboard downstairs. If someone needs to get something out of the closet, they'll ask you to get it for them, OK?"

"All right." Ella wondered if she should take notes. All this was coming rather fast.

"Good. Over that way is the boys' wing. You probably won't have to go there, at least not at night." A man emerged from the hallway and Tori smiled at him. "Hey Harold, this is Ella. She's going to be helping me out for awhile as an intern." Harold nodded.

"Hi, I'm one of the aides for the older guys around here. It's nice to meet you."

"You too." Ella shook his hand and followed Tori around to the other hallway.

"This is the girls' wing. How about we see if any of them are in so you can get to know them a little?"

"That sounds like a good idea."

Tori nodded matter-of-factly and knocked on the first door. There was a hand-drawn sign on it that read *Lisa, Maggie, Alison and Veronica* in colorful script.

From inside the door a bored voice called out, "Come in."

Tori pushed the door open and Ella stepped up behind her to see a spare room with two bunk beds, two dressers and a shelf. Two of the girls sat on the floor between the beds; one was braiding the other's hair. Another was reading on one of the top bunks.

"Hi there. This is Ella. She's a new intern." The girls nodded blandly.

"Ella, this is Lisa, Alison and Veronica. I'm not sure where Maggie went."

"She went to try and find more Kleenex — we're out," Veronica informed her.

"OK, see you." Tori closed their door and crossed the hall to another one. They made their way down the hall in this way, stopping at every door to be introduced to the inhabitants. None of them seemed very interested in Ella and some weren't even in their rooms. Finally they came to the last room on the left. The sign read *Brooke, Leann and Gabby*, and there were a lot of polka dots around the names. Then Ella saw it: under the other three names someone had written in 'Sabrina' with a marker, very small. It was almost unnoticeable.

Ella only had time to brace herself before the door was sliding open and four girls came into sight. Two of them were seated on one of the lower bunks doing homework and the other two hung upside down from the other bunk. One of these was petite with bright red hair and the other had serious gray eyes, which widened in shock when Ella stepped into view.

"Hi guys, this is Ella, she's our new intern. Ella, those two are Leanne and Brooke and over here are Gabby and Sabrina." She didn't say anything about the girls' peculiar position; she just closed the door again.

"There, I think that's everything. This room," she jabbed her thumb over her shoulder to the last door in the hallway, "is empty. Sabrina just came in a few days ago so she got put in with that threesome. Our next arrivals will go in here, but we can hope that they won't come along for a while."

As they walked back up the hallway, Tori turned to Ella and fixed her with a serious stare. "There's one thing you need to know. Under no circumstances are you to ask any of these kids about their lives or their families or how they got here. You have an obligation to listen if they want tell you, but it's not your place to nose in their business, OK?"

"I understand." Ella understood a whole lot more than Tori could ever know.

"All right then, I think that's all you need to see. If you have any questions don't bother asking Ben, he doesn't know anything. Just go directly to Harold or me. If neither of us is around ask two of the kids. Ask two different kids separately because they love to play tricks on you. Oh, yeah, and there are bathrooms just downstairs across the hall from the playroom. You don't get on shift for another forty-five minutes so if I were you, I'd walk around and acquaint yourself with some of the kids."

"Thanks for showing me around." Ella smiled and Tori smiled back, looking a bit more friendly this time. "No problem."

Ella did her best to follow Tori's advice but it was rather difficult because the only one of the children she actually wanted to talk to was Sabrina. She was also aware that Dawn and the others were waiting and sure to be somewhat anxious.

Ella went down to the kitchen again in time to see the last of the volunteers arrive. She swallowed and decided to avoid suspicion by ducking into the small lounge. There she found that the two boys she'd seen earlier had left, but the girl was still there, bent over a book. A friend seemed to have joined her. Ella recognized her from one of the dorm rooms.

"Hi there!" She did her best to sound cheerful. The girls looked up. Ella tried again. "I met you earlier; what's your name again?"

"Maya."

"And you are…?" Ella looked questioningly at the first girl.

"Louise." They didn't seem to be too keen on talking but Ella sat down next to them anyway.

"What are you two studying?"

"Math. We're learning about decimals."

"Cool. What grade are you in?"

"Sixth."

Ella realized this was getting nowhere and these weren't the people she wanted to see so she stood up. "It's nice to meet you. I'm sure I'll get to know you both better once I've been here awhile." The girls watched her as she left, raising their eyebrows at one another behind her back.

38

Sabrina looked up as the door opened. Tori stood there, all pink T-shirt and blonde hair but behind her was a face she recognized. Ella made no move of recognition as Tori introduced them. Sabrina pretended to mumble hello nonchalantly from her awkward position with her feet wedged under the other bed rail. Gabby smiled, looking almost too pleased. Brooke and Leann merely nodded. The door closed and Sabrina sat up, pulling with only her stomach. She stared at the wall beside Gabby's bed. What on earth were they thinking? Any plan they might have was not going to fly here.

Sabrina had seen the lengths the staff went to make sure that everyone was safely inside the orphanage. Regardless of how stupid this attempt might turn out to be, Sabrina knew Dawn would never settle for anything short of a perfect plan when it came to a rescue. So what could they be up to? Sabrina hoped it wouldn't get her in even more trouble than she was already in. Since she'd arrived three days ago, police had questioned her twice. Neither time had she felt the lies she told were very convincing.

Gabby started pulling on Sabrina's toes; she'd clambered up onto the upper bunk as well and was doing her best to pull Sabrina out of her pondering.

"You look totally gloomy. What's wrong?" Too often in the last few days Sabrina had found herself wanting to strangle the energetic redhead. This was one of these times.

"I'm fine. I'm just... thinking, that's all."

"You sure do think a lot." Despite herself, Sabrina found that rather funny.

"Yeah, I guess I do." She turned over and swung her torso over the edge of the bed, grabbing the slats beneath, just as Gabby had done on Sabrina's first day. She flipped over and let herself down gently on the mattress beneath.

"I'm going to the bathroom," she announced. She had decided on one thing. She had to talk to Ella and find out what on earth the Barn Brigade had dreamed up. Sabrina left the room and looked to the end of the hall. Ella and Tori had gone. She trotted down the hall and turned the corner, taking the stairs two at a time. After a quick scan of the younger children's play area and the aides' room Sabrina checked the women's bathroom. No one was in there either. She bumped into Tori on her way out but Ella was no longer with her.

"Hello there!" Tori smiled and Sabrina nodded a response as she let the door fall shut behind her. Tori had been especially kind to Sabrina ever since she'd come. Sabrina had the feeling Tori saw it as her duty to try and make up for the horrible lives of the children she took care of. It was likely that Tori had no idea what it was like to be them, to actually have all their problems, but it was a nice gesture nonetheless.

Sabrina slipped through the lobby, avoiding looking at Ben, and started down the stairs that lead to the kitchen and the lounge. Ella was walking towards her. As soon as she saw her, Ella looked covertly over each shoulder. No one was coming. She held up one finger and put her hand into her bag.

"You're Sabrina, right?" Ella moved towards her pulling something from her bag. Sabrina recognized the bag, and the trick Ella was using. Anyone overhearing their conversation would think they were just meeting for the first time. She played along with it; Ella wasn't the one she was mad at.

"Yeah, that's me."

Ella handed her something. A letter. Sabrina slipped it under her shirt and into the waistband of her sweatpants.

"I'm looking forward to getting to know you and the others while I'm working here."

"Good luck. I'm told we can be a handful." Sabrina gave a furtive *what's going on?* look, and Ella gestured to Sabrina's midriff where the letter was stowed.

"Thanks, I'm not sure yet if I'll need it but it's good to know at least some of you are on my side."

They heard footsteps near the bottom of the stairs and Ella winced as she started to pass Sabrina on the stairs. "It's good to talk to you. I'll try my best to remember your name."

Over Ella's shoulder, Sabrina saw Harold approach and hastily made as if she was preparing to leave. "OK, I'll see you then." Sabrina smiled over her shoulder at Ella so she wouldn't have to adjust her expression for Harold.

Ella nodded and continued up the stairs past Sabrina, who was left to scurry down the stairs. Sabrina tried not to freeze as she passed Harold. He looked so knowing and amused she found it difficult to act normal. Sabrina stepped down one stair, then another, pretending to have lost her train of thought. Harold looked at her and opened his mouth to speak. In that instant, Sabrina knew she was doomed, Ella was doomed, whatever scheme they had cooked up was doomed and then...

"It's so nice that you're getting to know Ella. She does seem like an agreeable person, doesn't she?" Sabrina nodded and, relieved, brushed past the aide, turning left at the bottom of the staircase into the lounge near the kitchen. There were two younger girls in there already so Sabrina pretended to look for something, raising her hands in mock frustration when she failed to find the imaginary object. She left the room before either of the others could pose a question. There was a small unisex bathroom for the volunteers to use near the kitchen. Sabrina darted inside and locked the door. The children weren't allowed to use this bathroom but she figured it was safer than trying to read the letter in her dorm room or anywhere else. She opened the paper, ripping the tape a little in her haste and pulled the two sheets of paper apart to read. They were in Ella's handwriting.

Dear Sabrina,

We don't presume to know the reason that you ran away, or whether you wish to return or not, but before you decide I want to tell you something. Dawn told us her story. She's very sorry for everything she put you through and wants you back here as much as any of us. We don't know what we're going to do about the problem with Alyssa yet, but you can trust that something will be done. I want to make sure you remember every part of the plan, so please read this aloud to yourself if you can. Your plan is as follows:

Sabrina read aloud in a faint whisper the instructions Ella had written down.

Sometime later tonight, preferably right as everyone is going to bed, but not asleep, I want to you to fake respiratory distress. Do whatever you want, but just nothing that could be treated by primary first aid, so no choking. An extreme asthma attack is what we came up with, but if you can think of something better, please do that instead. Do this where at least one person can see you, they'll run for help. Here's where the risk comes in. Basically we won't have time to wait for an ambulance so you'll be entrusted to me, and I'll drive you to the 'hospital' if everything works out.

I'll let you out at Orswyn Park where the others are waiting and you'll stay there as I return to the orphanage. The lie is that you were faking the asthma attack, and as soon as I opened the door, you took off and I couldn't catch you. Please know that every single one of us is really, really sorry you felt hurt enough to run away— especially Dawn. We want you back so we'll try our very best to make sure this plan works. Tessa wants me to tell you that she loves you and I'm seconding that on behalf of the rest of the Barn Brigade. I'm so glad I'll get to see you again soon; you caused a major pity party by leaving like that. Good luck on your part,
Love,
Ella.
P.S. Get rid of this letter; if anyone reads it we're finished.

Sabrina blinked back tears; she tore up the letter into small pieces and dropped them into the toilet. She'd been so mad but now there was nothing left, nothing but an empty space where her anger had been, that was now filling up with regret. She pressed the lever and the pieces of Ella's letter swirled down the drain. Sabrina knew what she was going to do. She had to follow Ella's plan. She only hoped they wouldn't get caught.

Sabrina slipped out of the bathroom without being noticed and ran up the stairs and through the lobby without incident. It was only when she came to the playroom that she encountered trouble. Gabby was waiting outside the door to the girl's bathroom. She looked confused when she saw Sabrina.

"I thought you said you were using the bathroom."

"I was." It wasn't actually a lie; she'd used the bathroom, just not in the usual way.

"Then why were you out there?" Gabby made a pouty face.

"I went to the downstairs bathroom."

"That's not allowed."

"I know, but the little girls were having a meetup in here and I didn't want to interrupt them."

Gabby's face lit up. "I remember those! We used to congregate in the bathrooms whenever one of us had a problem and talk it over."

"Exactly." Sabrina wasn't really listening but she followed the younger girl upstairs anyway.

39

Even though Dawn had had to be sly, invisible, or convincing dozens of times, this was definitely the most important. She sat with Rita in the playground's tunnel. Tessa and Alyssa shared the playhouse. No one had spoken in hours. Each was too absorbed in her own thoughts and worries to speak. No one wanted to be the one to shatter the dubious silence.   Dawn closed her eyes. There was no use getting nervous this early. The sun wasn't even all the way down yet. She opened one eye to check her watch. Seven thirty-five. The orphanage kids were probably all eating dinner right about now. Come to think of it, someone could have gone in as a volunteer to help Ella. But no, Sabrina was probably still furious with Dawn and Alyssa, and anyway, if Alyssa were spotted, they'd probably take her in to live there. Tessa looked exactly like Sabrina, so that was no good, and Rita had spent a few months there waiting for her moms to get back from Uganda. Oh well, it was too late for that now.

      Dawn wondered about Rita's moms. The truth was they were probably dead or in prison. Even if they weren't, even if they did come back, Rita would probably never find out. It made Dawn sad, sad enough to delve into memories of her own mother, and the day they found out that her dad had jumped off a bridge. How much she had cried, how she'd held her brother when he screamed at night. Her mother hadn't comforted them much. She'd locked herself in her study without a word. Dawn never knew why she secluded herself, why she never shed a tear, why she refused to organize a funeral, why she burned down her only tie to family. That was the largest question. Shouldn't losing someone make you value home and family more? And to try and kill her own children, and partly succeed.

Dawn's fists clenched and suddenly she was angry. Her own mother had left her in a burning house to die and what if her wish had been fulfilled? What if Dawn had died that night? Honestly, a few days ago Dawn wouldn't really have cared. She frowned. Had she really been transformed over a single night? Did she really care about her life now, or had she cared all along and only just realized it? She bit her lip and let her fists relax. Ella was right. She had been stupid to try and kill herself. She was the one always telling the others not to give up. True, she'd been referring to physical exertion, or clandestine robbery stratagems, but didn't the same principles apply?

Dawn felt a sudden surge of gratitude towards Ella. In her view, Ella had saved her life. It was true that Dawn had not wanted saving at the moment. A number of times she'd tried and failed, freezing with a knife to her throat, or hesitating with the climbing rope around her neck. Dawn could count every single attempt and hoped with all her heart that this latest would be her last. Was it just the influence her father had left? Dawn had never relished pain and found it absurd that someone would choose a method of suicide as painful as jumping off a bridge. She'd always tried for something less intimidating. At least, she'd hoped for a painless exit. Maybe those who did choose painful methods thought they deserved it. Dawn never thought she deserved to live, but to die in pain was not part of the bargain.

Dawn had seen articles urging you to talk to someone if you even 'think about suicide'. It was a bad way to put it; doesn't everyone think about suicide? Maybe fairly few contemplate actually committing it. And why use the word *commit*? To commit to something meant to pledge to an act, but Dawn had a feeling this word had affiliations with the other meaning of *commit*. To commit a crime — but was it really a crime if you perpetrated it on yourself? Dawn had committed hundreds of robberies and thefts for personal gain and always hated herself for doing so. It was what had become necessary, but she'd never found herself enjoying it. Guilt had subsided over the years to make way for a bleak acceptance. Dawn found herself aware of her crimes but detached from their consequences. Somehow that made her feel a little less human, and that thought made her hopelessly sad.

40

The dinner bell rang, and Gabby took off. Sabrina could've sworn she completely disappeared for a second, until her own arm was practically yanked off as the energetic redhead grabbed onto Sabrina and dragged her off downstairs for spaghetti and salad.

Sabrina caught sight of Ella standing near Tori and nodding slowly to whatever she was saying. The two took a slow headcount and when they seemed sure that more than half of the children were present, Tori gave the thumbs-up to one of the volunteers and the line began to move. Sabrina was served spaghetti but refused the meatballs; she had been a barn-enforced vegetarian for too long for them to look appetizing.

Gabby led her to what had become their usual table at the far end of the hall and they sat together as they ate. Sabrina was lost in thought. How exactly did someone fake an asthma attack? She'd witnessed one once, in second grade, when a boy called Will had begun wheezing and coughing and had to be taken to the hospital by the music teacher, but she was not quite prepared to replicate it.

Gabby tried several times to engage her in conversation but Sabrina repelled her attempts. She didn't want this annoying little girl interrupting her planning.

Gabby noticed Sabrina's unsociable behavior almost immediately and commented on it, putting her head down near the table to try and get a look into Sabrina's downcast eyes. "What's wrong?"

"Nothing." Sabrina tried to avert the question to no avail.

"Are you sure?"

"Yeah…"

"Something's wrong; you can't fool me."

"I'm fine, I'm just thinking."

"What about?"

Honestly, Sabrina thought, this girl never shuts up. With a sigh, she relented. "I'm trying to figure out how to factor a polynomial." There. That ought to keep her quiet for while.

Over at the staff table, Ella was having a terrible time socializing. Tori, Ben and Harold were all there along with a few other people who ran the laundry and food coordination. Ella smiled as much as she could and tried to laugh with them as she was introduced over and over again. All the people were older than her. Tori had taken this as a full-time job right after she graduated from college. The others were all older than her. They finally seized on Ella's college education for subject matter.

"What are you studying? Do you have a major yet?" Ella though it best to be as truthful as possible.

"I'm majoring in engineering and mechanics. I'm very good with electrical and mechanical stuff."

Tori laughed, "Good! That means you can help fix our problem with the oven."

Ella looked suspicious. "What's wrong with the oven?"

"Its light flickers on and off continuously."

"Is that it?"

"Yeah."

Ella smirked; this was a whole lot easier than she hade anticipated. "I'm pretty sure I can fix that. I'd have to look at it though."

Harold nodded. "Of course, but not now."

Ella shook her head. "No, I'm still eating. This is good food!"

"Be sure to thank the volunteers then, they usually enjoy praise. It's mostly church groups trying to encourage their congregations to be charitable, but at least the kids get food."

Ella nodded with a forced sympathetic smile.

After dinner most of the children traipsed back to their respective rooms or quarters to begin their homework. Sabrina did her best to ignore Gabby's antics as the younger girl procrastinated on her work. She had a habit of kicking the wall, which drove Sabrina bonkers. Sabrina concentrated on her breathing, trying to figure out how she could make a wheezing sound without actually hurting herself. She was having a hard time keeping her attempts quiet, and Brooke and Leann kept looking at her weirdly. Still, it was better if they thought she's already been breathing badly.

Gabby thrust her head over the rail, letting her voluminous red hair fall down around it. "Hey Sabrina, what's nine times twenty-eight?" Of course, Sabrina didn't know off the top of her head, it took her a few seconds to work it out, as well, but Gabby seemed mightily impressed when Sabrina provided the answer. "Two hundred fifty-two... I think."

"Thanks!" Gabby's head retracted and Sabrina rolled her eyes as she went back to her wheezing practice. Her nerves about tonight were mounting with every irritating tick of the clock. What made it worse was that she knew there had to be spectators. She wasn't sure if she could fool anyone.

Ella followed Tori into the girls' dormitory. There were maybe twenty miniature cots and ten slightly larger ones. Little girls in various stages of donning their pajamas scurried around looking for toothbrushes and brushing hair. One started crying because one of her socks had gone missing and Tori told Ella to help her find it.

"Just look under her bed and the dresser. She's bound to have misplaced it somewhere."

Ella did as she was told, patting the kindergartner on the back as she bent down to search beneath the bed.

"I already looked there, it's goooone!" She began to wail again and Ella pulled back the covers on her cot, revealing the little blue sock crumpled into a ball.

"There you go, I found it for you!" The little girl looked up at Ella with streaming eyes and sniffed.

Tori swooped on them. "What do you say, Angela?"

Angela shuffled her feet, one still sockless. "Thank you very much."

Ella gave her a big smile. "You're welcome."

Tori gave Ella a thumbs-up as they turned back to the rest of the room. "OK, you all ready to brush you teeth?"

The girls filed out behind Tori with Ella taking up the rear. They brushed their teeth, taking turns at the three sinks. It took quite a while but when everyone was done and had used the bathroom and brushed their hair and generally gotten ready for bed, Tori ushered them back across the hall to their dormitory. Ella saw Harold and another man she hadn't yet met just bringing their horde of little boys, pushing and shoving, out of the boy's bathroom. Tori opened the door to the dorm again and everyone finally began to settle down. There was a total of seven nightlights in the dorm and all of them went on as soon as Tori turned off the light. She closed the door behind them and turned to Ella.

"That's them taken care of. Please stay down here in case any of them has some sort of problem. I'm going to get the older girls down here to brush their teeth. They take a whole lot longer because they like to wash their faces and floss and stuff. Some of them take showers at night too, so they go by rooms, with three rooms in there at a time."

Ella nodded. She could handle waiting here for a while. Once Sabrina began her act, everyone would know about it. Ella took up her position in the aides' room and brought out her textbook to avoid suspicion. She read the first line and decided it was boring so continued to stare at it without actually reading until the first child tugged at her sleeve.

It was a boy, about four years old.

"Can I have some water? I'm thirsty."

Ella smiled. "Certainly, but what's the magic word?"

"Please?"

Ella took out a paper cup and filled it from the water filter on the desk. "There you go, sleep well!"

"Thanks." The kid waddled away with his drink and Ella went back to pretending to do homework. The words had long since lost meaning to her and she let her mind wander freely as the minutes ticked by.

"Hey, Ella!" it was Harold, tapping on her shoulder. She turned to look at him.

"Yeah?"

"I'll take a turn down here. Can you go help supervise the bathroom rotation? Apparently it gets kind of hectic over on the girls' end."

"OK, sure." She stood up and put her book back in the bag, slinging the latter over her shoulder.

"You can leave that here; there's nowhere else to dump it." Ella hesitated, but there was nothing incriminating in her bag so she let it go and set it down by the wastebasket.

"See you later!"

Ella nodded and slipped into the bathroom. Whoever had told Harold it was hectic had been right. The showers consisted of six heads coming out of the walls in a small tiled room about three feet by eight feet with no curtains or anything. Some girls wore swimsuits but others just didn't care anymore. Five girls were showering as Ella entered. Four were grouped around the sinks brushing hair and teeth and washing faces. The remaining three must have been inside the toilet stalls. There was no giggling or happy jokes being told as there might be in a similar set-up on a school trip. These girls were sisters, in effect; there was nothing special about each others' company anymore. There was more bickering than merry-making. Ella assumed that was why she was there, to stop things from slowing down if the girls got preoccupied with which washcloth belonged to whom, though in actuality she had no idea.

A girl in green stripy pajamas stepped out of one of the stalls and added to the chaos at the sinks as she attempted to wash her hands. Tori opened the door and stepped in.

"Oh Ella, Harold sent you in here? Good, good. That means I can monitor the others upstairs without having to run up and down every five seconds to make sure this lot isn't loitering." She gave the girls a mockingly stern look and left the bathroom.

After everyone had had their turn in the bathroom and toted their things back to their respective rooms Ella returned to the aides' room where she'd left Harold. He was no longer there. His assistant sat at the desk, carelessly paging through a garden catalogue. He looked up as Ella approached.

"Hello, you're Ella, aren't you? Good to meet you. I don't think we've been introduced, I'm Rick." He went on without drawing breath. "Harold put me on duty here. Are you coming with a message?"

Ella shook her head. "I was here before Harold so I thought he might want me to take over. Do you need any help?"

"No, no. I'm fine, go about your merry business, please."

Ella, slightly taken aback, nevertheless took him up on it and left the room. She climbed the stairs carefully to find Tori and Harold seated at the table in the room above.

"Hey." Harold followed Tori's gaze.

"Rick sent you up?"

"Yeah. A very interesting fellow."

Harold snickered, "Indeed."

Tori stood up. "I guess I'll show you the lights-out procedure, just so you can do it on your own if you have to." She led Ella down the girls' hallway. "You've probably noticed that the rooms go from oldest to youngest. We start at the end and turn out their lights a little bit later as we get to the older girls' rooms. Does that make sense?"

Ella nodded even though it didn't, and watched as Tori knocked on the door to the last door on the left.

"Come in." It was a carefree voice, belonging to the redheaded girl Ella had seen earlier. Tori pushed open the door. Brooke and Leann were each on their respective bunks acting slightly high and mighty while Sabrina helped Gabby to tuck the sheets back over the end of her bed. Ella wondered vaguely why Sabrina was in a younger girls' room, probably just because it was the only one open at the time. That was of little importance now.

"You guys OK in here?" Brooke and Leanne nodded dutifully and Gabby nodded gleefully. Sabrina refused to comment. "That's good then. I'm going to turn the lights out, so get in bed."

Sabrina obliged, flopping onto her lower bunk and wriggling under the blanket. Gabby was less obedient, she was still on the ladder up to her bed and tugging on the sheet.

"Can you help me with this? It won't stay put!" Tori gave Ella a subtle nudge and Gabby watched gratefully as the older girl tucked the fitted sheet carefully under the end of the mattress.

"How's that?"

"That's fabulous!"

Ella smiled at her ridiculous word choice and took her place once more behind Tori. Gabby pulled her blanket up to her chin and settled in as Tori clicked off the light and closed the door.

41

Sabrina decided to activate the plan after everyone had gone to bed, but before they were asleep, just as the letter suggested. As soon as the aides had gone she began, slowly and carefully faking a soft wheeze and an occasional cough.

A street lamp shone through the fluttering curtains, creating weird shadows every time the curtains moved. There was so much light, Sabrina could have read. She cleared her throat loudly and rolled over. As she came to face the wall a small hand descended into view from the bunk above, connected to an arm in red pajamas, holding a pen and a note. Sabrina checked the other bed. Brooke's eyes were closed and Leanne was facing the other way. She took the note. It was not the best idea because she couldn't very well go into respiratory distress while passing notes without her asking about it prematurely and getting the aides. Still, Sabrina was intrigued, any kind of note always got her curious. Telling herself she wouldn't reply, she tugged the scrap of paper from Gabby's hand and read the messy sentence on it.

I'm wide awake; will you tell me a story?

Sabrina did not want to tell her a story, but it was good that she was wide awake. This way Sabrina was guaranteed a witness. She looked up and grudgingly took the pen that Gabby still held.

A thought akin to *oh, good grief* crossed Sabrina's mind. Now she was really in a mess, it was going to be difficult to get out of this one now. She quickly scribbled a message on the back of the note.

I'm tired; you should sleep too.

It was the classic excuse but she sent it anyway and handed the pen back up with it. In a few moments Gabby's hand appeared again.

Please? I won't sleep until you tell me a story.

Fine then, don't sleep.

Sabrina felt a little bad about her snappy tone, but it was in her best interest right now to make sure she had no conversation that could potentially ruin her escape.

That's not very nice.

I don't care, I'm trying to sleep.

Sabrina kept up her consistent wheeze, it was starting to hurt her throat. Gabby's response came quickly, and Sabrina almost groaned aloud when she saw it.

Please tell me a story. Tell me how you know Ella.

Sabrina gaped at the darkness, she pinched herself, just to be sure, but she was definitely conscious.

What are you talking about? I don't know Ella.

You're lying.

No I'm not.

Yes you are, now tell me.

No.

Yes.

What makes you think I know her?

The look on your face, plus you told me you went to the downstairs bathroom but Tori saw you coming out of the upstairs one before I arrived and Harold said you were talking to her so I just kind of guessed. I'm right, aren't I?

No.

You're lying, aren't you?

175

Sabrina had never felt more stupid in her entire life. She took the pen and scribbled a response.

It's none of your business. Go to sleep.

No, I won't sleep until you tell me. You could also tell me why you ran away from home.

How do you know I ran away? That's supposed to be confidential.

I overheard Ben talking to one of those policemen.

Sabrina was overwhelmed. What was this, the Social Services Inquisition? It was just too much. To be blackmailed by a redheaded twelve-year-old? But was this blackmail? Gabby hadn't said anything about telling people about it if Sabrina didn't enlighten her. Still, Sabrina didn't want to take the risk.

You shouldn't eavesdrop.

Sorry.

Sabrina was dumbfounded; she didn't even deny it.

You better be. So I ran away, so what? I bet a lot of people here did.

Yeah, but they don't like to talk about it.

Neither do I.

Why not?

Sabrina rubbed her forehead and coughed for the third time in ten minutes. What should she tell this nosy orphan? At last she decided to be truthful, if stiff.

Fine, I have a sister and I miss her, that's all.

What's her name?

Tessa.

Why didn't she run away with you?

It's none of your business.

That doesn't mean I don't want to know.

Sabrina had to think for a second before responding.

I didn't invite her, that's why she stayed behind.

What, with your terrible parents?

Stop it. There's a reason I didn't tell you all this, you know.

And what's that?

So you wouldn't ask me all these questions. How did you get here anyway?

There was a slight sigh from the upper bunk as Gabby read the note. For a moment, Sabrina though she wasn't going to answer, she coughed twice before the hand appeared again.

I'd really rather tell you out loud. It's so much easier than passing notes up and down.

Sabrina experienced a rush of annoyance. If all went well she wouldn't even be here tomorrow. It seemed, however, that the question had thrown Gabby, putting up her guard a little so Sabrina tried again.

OK then, you can tell me tomorrow. Let's both get some sleep.

Not so fast. You still haven't told me your story.

A new ploy occurred to Sabrina and she made quick work of it. *You wouldn't believe me if I told you.*

I would if you told the truth.

And how'd you make sure of that?

I'm smart.

Smart wasn't exactly the word Sabrina would have used, but she let it slide.

Fine then, I'll tell you.

Really?

No.

Why not?

Because it's a sensitive topic that's not actually any of your business.

My story isn't any of your business either.

OK then, don't tell me.

I want to tell you.

Then tell me now.

OK.

Really?

Yeah.

Go on then.

The next note took a little longer in coming, and when Gabby finally lowered it through the crack between wall and bed it was covered with scratchings-out and false starts. It seemed that, for all her nonchalance and eagerness, this subject still held some pain for her. Finally halfway down there was a single sentence.

I was raised by a single mother. An insane murderer killed her.

Sabrina was shocked. Maybe it was the lack of detail or the fact that it was on paper, not in words that would linger with her until her final hour, but even with the number of depressing stories she had heard, even with the one she'd lived, she found it hard to comprehend how Gabby must have suffered. She put pen to paper very carefully and handed back her message.

I'm very sorry. I'm amazed you wanted to tell me. I'm flattered that you trust me. My story isn't nearly that dramatic.

Then can you tell me about it?

Guilt trip. Sabrina chewed a strand of her hair and finally wrote.

Fine. My parents divorced after beating each other up for years. Tessa and I tricked them both into thinking we were living with the other one and ran away. You happy?

There was a moment where Gabby must've absorbed the information then another note arrived.

That's not all.

It wasn't a question and Sabrina was annoyed that the younger girl had noticed.

How do you know that?

Easy. Earlier you said you left Tessa behind, and just now you said she went with you. She's not here now, so where'd you leave her?

Was this girl an orphan or an FBI agent? Sabrina felt bad for thinking it, but still there are lines one does not cross with someone she met three days ago. Sabrina established this loud and clear with her next message.

I'm not telling you.
Yes you are.
Why?
Because you're a nice person.

Inexplicably, Sabrina's eyes filled with tears. She had always been known as the mean one, the control freak who kept her sister under her black leathery wing all the time and never let her out to breathe. Some people in elementary school had even called her the "evil twin." There was no way Gabby would think she was nice if Tess was around. Still, she wasn't sure she wanted to be thought well of by a twelve year-old energetic blackmailer. She wasn't sure how to put that all into words, or even if she wanted to, so she settled for: *No, I'm not.*

Yes you are. I know you are.

Let me guess; because you're smart?

That's right. Now tell me your secret before I guess.

I don't care if you guess.

OK then. I'd say you were hiding out in a barn somewhere for a while. With Ella and Tessa. Am I right?

What in the name of trail mix did this girl do in her spare time? Still, Sabrina wasn't going to give up that easily.

What makes you think that?

You'll be mad at me if I say.

I'm already mad at you.

OK. It's the way you guys smell.

What!?

Ella smells like old hay. You smelled the same when you arrived.

Sabrina had to hand it to her. *You're going to be a brilliant detective.*

Thanks. So why is Ella here?

I don't know.

You're lying.

How do you always know? And don't just say you're smart.

Your handwriting slants more when you lie. When you're talking you always scratch your nose if you're saying something unconvincing.

Sabrina already knew about the nose thing. Tessa had figured it out years ago and ever since she'd been trying to correct the habit, but even Tessa hadn't noticed the handwriting.

Fine, I'm lying, but I wouldn't lie if I wanted to tell you.

Fine then, I'll guess again.

Don't!

Too late. I think Ella and Tessa have some hare-brained scheme to get you out of here involving your obviously false wheezing. Is that right?

No, it's not right. Sabrina made sure her writing was completely perpendicular to the bottom of the page. As she gritted her teeth in offense and shame.

You're lying again. You over-corrected the slant.

That's literally freaky.

Thanks. You were going to wait until I was almost asleep and then fake an asthma attack, weren't you? Sorry, but that's utterly ill-conceived and doomed to fail.

I know. Don't rub it in.

How are you going to get back to the barn? Ella has to work. And what if someone else takes you to the hospital?

I've been thinking about this all day, I don't need you to get me all nervous again. Not that this plan will work anymore now that you know about it.

Who said anything about that? All you need is an accomplice.

Are you volunteering?

On one condition.

No.

You don't even know what it is yet.

I still say no, I won't be able to do anything for you once I'm back at home.

I know; that's why I want to go with you.

Of all the crazy things Gabby had written that night, this was the worst. Sabrina toed the edge of the mattress as she thought how to reply. She chose the simple option.

No.

Fine, I'll tell them all about you.

That's blackmail.

Isn't it fun?

No.

So you'll take me with you.

I'll see what the others think once you help me escape. Is that good enough for you?

No.

I'm supposed to say that.

You have to make sure to meet me in the alley behind that weird old restaurant; it's only a few blocks from my school.

And when are we to do this, O queen?

Tomorrow at four fifteen.

I'll see what I can do. But bring your own clothes; I don't want to have to steal more for you.

You steal?

Yes. Are you still sure you want to come?

Now I want to come even more.

Kleptomaniac.

What does that mean?

It's someone who is obsessed with stealing things.

I'm not obsessed.

I'll be the judge of that.

Sabrina was not happy with this. Another known-to-be-missing child was all the Barn Brigade needed right now; but Gabby would be useful with that know-it-all detective talent of hers. Sabrina was genuinely impressed; this tiny girl had gotten more information out of her in half an hour than the cops had managed in three days.

So, now that you've got me, let's get started!

You sure?

Yeah. It's now or never.

That sound so cliché. Whatever, I'll start once Ella's on guard. Can you check?

Sure!

Gabby slipped out of bed and crept to the door, opening it a tiny bit and peeking through the narrow yellow gap to see who was on guard. A moment later she turned around and gave Sabrina a gleeful thumbs-up.

42

Ella was tense, waiting for any sign of noise, any signaling scream, or thunderous cough from Sabrina's room. She sat hunched at the table in the space separating the boys' wing from the girls' wing. She hadn't moved in half an hour, since Tori had set her here. Ella had pretended to read for a while, but soon found that too stressful to be worth it. Now she simply listened, trying not to think about all the possibilities for defeat.

It happened quite suddenly. The door at the end of the hall banged open and the small redheaded girl — Gabby — came hurtling along the corridor. Behind her Ella could hear sounds of uncontrollable coughing. A little light of hope opened inside her as Gabby grabbed her arm.

"Come quick! Sabrina can't breathe!"

Ella ran after the girl, trying to act her part as she reached the door. It wasn't difficult. Sabrina was huddled on her bed pretending to gasp for air while her slightly panicked eyes darted over Ella's face. She made eye contact for a fraction of a second before Ella was beside her.

"Gabby, go get Tori or one of the other aides now!" Ella decided it was best to pretend to follow the asthma routine she'd learned when she took First Aid. "Can you speak?"

Sabrina grabbed at her trachea and managed to fake a strangled "Not... really." from her supposedly constricted throat.

"Has this ever happened to you before?" Ella knew it hadn't, but all this was for Brooke and Leann's benefit; they were awake and huddled together on Brooke's bed whispering worriedly.

Sabrina shook her head and went into another false coughing fit. There were footsteps from outside and Gabby burst in with Tori and Rick on her heels.

"What's going on?" Rick demanded, striding over to examine Sabrina.

"I think it's asthma, though she said it's never happened before," Ella told him. "I think she should go to the ER."

"Yeah," Tori cut in, "I'll call 911." She made to rise, but Ella stopped her. "There's not enough time for that. I can drive her."

Tori hesitated for a moment before she gave in. "OK, I'll come too. Rick, please get these girls back to bed."

Rick nodded solemnly and stepped to the side as Tori leaned in to question Sabrina again. "Can you stand?"

Sabrina tried to pull herself from the bed. Ella grabbed one of her friend's shoulders and hauled her up. On the inside Ella was panicking. One of the many flaws in their plan was unfolding. How was she going to let Sabrina out of the car without Tori noticing? And if she managed that, how would she stop Tori from calling the police? There was no time to think, and Ella was too frazzled with keeping up her act to work out a plan, let alone a way to convey it to Sabrina. With Tori on Sabrina's other side, the trio moved swiftly through the dorm, stopping to let Sabrina cough at the top of the stairs. Harold intercepted them.

"What's going on?" He looked from the panting Sabrina to the two slightly panicked women with a worried expression.

"Ask Rick, he's upstairs. We're taking Sabrina to the hospital." With that, Ella pushed past Harold, dragging her two companions with her as they hurried downstairs. Ella snatched her bag from the aides' room and rushed them on towards the front door. Tori punched in a code on the lock, which made Ella suddenly glad they hadn't decided to break in instead. The night air hit them in the face and Ella found herself shivering as they staggered to the van. Sabrina was lifted into the back seat and Tori made to get in after her. Thinking quickly, Ella put her best interests into action, trying to convey with her eyes what the Sabrina should do.

"Wait, Tori. Don't you think she should lie down? Sabrina, would it feel good to lie down?" Ella nodded her head a fraction of an inch to indicate that the younger girl should answer in the affirmative. Either Sabrina got the message, or she really did want to lie down, either way, she managed to nod between coughs.

Tori nodded as well. "All right then." She climbed into the front seat with Ella and they took off. Ella's mind raced as she pulled along the darkened streets. She had no choice but to head for the hospital, but she'd made sure Sabrina was alone in the back seat, so if she figured out how to make a break for it, she could.

43

Sabrina's lungs were actually starting to hurt by the time the car started to move. Nevertheless, she kept up her act, as to fail at that was to admit defeat, an instinct Dawn had drilled out of her months ago. She lay on her side as the van sped through downtown Redfield, trying desperately to think of a plan. She'd never been in this situation before, completely trapped by those who were trying to help her. At least Ella was on her side, even if neither of them could let on. And now she had Gabby to fall back on as well.

There was no way she could have slowed her heartbeat down without breaking her persistent wheeze, but at least she felt a bit easier knowing that. Easy enough to free her mind from hysteria long enough to concoct a plot. If she was too slow about it Tori would have time to call the police, but if she took too much advantage of any obvious opportunity, Tori might conclude that she and Ella were in cahoots. Still pretending to gasp for air, Sabrina elevated herself on an elbow and snuck a look into the front seat, just as she expected. Tori hadn't brought a bag with her. Now if her cell phone was in her pocket... that was another matter, but that was one doubt that Sabrina couldn't afford. Next her eyes flickered to the locks on the car door. The red stripe was showing, that was good. She wouldn't have to waste time unlocking the door if she made a break for it.

I'll go at the next red light, she promised herself. The next three lights were green, and Sabrina began to sweat as they moved farther and farther from Orswyn Park, where she wanted to be. She didn't want to be too near it when she ran; it was too obvious a hiding place. But if she was too far away she wouldn't be able to reach it before her legs gave out. This was all a careful balance, so as soon as the next red light came into view, Sabrina readied herself.

Ella braked the car in front of the light and Sabrina readied herself, covering her movements with a fresh outbreak of coughing. She grabbed hold of latch and waited until the last second. As Ella began to move forward once more, Sabrina sprang. She thrust her side into the door and jumped out, slamming the door behind her. She hit the ground running and took off at a sprint, not allowing herself to look back.

44

Ella heard the van door slam and took off towards the now-green traffic light. She didn't even register what had happened until Tori started yelling.

"Oh my God! She ran! Did you see?"

Ella waited until she was able to pull over to look. Sure enough, Sabrina was no longer in the back seat. She did her best to fake shock. "Wait, how? She was...Oh my God, she was faking that whole time, wasn't she?"

Tori nodded slowly, her eyes wide. "She must have been. But now what? What are we going to tell Harold and Rick, and Mr. Wallace?"

"The truth," Ella said simply.

"We'll be fired for sure. Why did she do it?"

"I don't know, but we should turn around. We can't let her get too far."

Tori seemed to remember what one is supposed to do in these circumstances. She reached tentatively for her pocket. "Oh, no. I don't have my phone on me. Do you?"

Ella did an inner fist-pump as she managed a wince on the outside. "No, sorry, we'll have to go right back if we want to phone the cops."

"Then let's go, the faster we get there, the less likely she is to get away."

Ella knew that, of course, and did her best to be slow as they went back, without letting on that she was manipulating the pace. She almost started to feel bad for Tori as they made their way back towards the orphanage. Tori wasn't supposed to be the victim of their plan. There wasn't meant to *be* a victim. The poor woman was only trying to do her job right. She was doing what she thought to be best for the children in her care, even if their wishes were to the contrary. Ella thought she could see a little bit of resentment in Tori's eyes as they finally stepped out of the van and trotted up to the orphanage door. Resentment for the ungratefulness Sabrina had shown by choosing the streets over her care. Resentment for the girl who she barely even knew, yet would probably succeed in making Tori lose her job.

They rang the bell and waited in tense silence as Rick rushed to the door, inquiring as to their identities through the intercom before opening the door to let them in. Harold was behind him.

"What's going on? Where's Sabrina? Why are you back so soon?" Harold demanded. Ella and Tori tried hurriedly to explain.

"She took off as we stopped at a red light. She was faking the asthma attack."

"Yeah, she jumped out and slammed the door."

Tori looked like she might cry. "It's not our fault, I swear! We came right back, so now we're going to call the police."

Ella nodded, feeling a slight prick that Tori had claimed it wasn't Ella's fault either. It always made her feel guilty and a little grateful when people lied for her, whether they knew they were doing it or not.

Harold led the way through a door to the right of the front desk, and the others followed him dubiously.

"We don't blame you." Rick told Ella as they went. "She was already a runaway. A lot of them don't like being taken in here. They feel like they're being captured, even if it's for their own good."

Ella gave a shuddering sigh and nodded. The room on the right turned out to be Mr. Wallace's office. On the desk were many papers, folders, pens, and other office materials, all arranged with haphazard abandon. In the middle of the mess sat a telephone, which Tori grabbed immediately, punching in 911 and holding the phone to her ear as she waited for the response.

Ella listened to Tori's side of the conversation, trying to avoid eye contact with anyone.

"Hi, um, I'm calling from the Social Services Center orphanage. We have a missing person… About half an hour ago. Sabrina Mantz. Yes, she was one of the children under our care. At the intersection of Stratwood and 59th street. We were taking her to the hospital, she'd been having… well, faking an asthma attack. No, one of my colleagues was with me… Yes, she has shoulder length dark brown hair and gray eyes. I think we have her exact height and weight on file, one moment." Tori's hands shook as she searched the desk frantically for the file she'd mentioned.

Behind her, Ella's ears pricked up. A file about Sabrina? That could be damaging if they looked through it enough. Finally, Tori found it and flipped it open to the first page within. "OK, she's five feet six inches, 123 pounds. Fourteen years old… OK, OK. That's fine. All right, thank you." Tori hung up the phone with a sigh of relief. "They're sending a squad out there now, hopefully they'll be able to catch her before she gets too far."

Ella made a point of visibly relaxing her shoulders as the others voiced their moderate relief. She tried to avoid openly staring at Sabrina's file, which still lay open on the desk, but found it extremely difficult. She made up her mind to look through it later on, provided she could do so without being caught.

45

Sabrina knew her way around the city pretty well. She at least knew how to get to the park Ella had mentioned, which was lucky. She also knew that she didn't have much time. She sprinted as fast as she could, going through alleys and parking lots when possible. If she could avoid being seen now, it would make it easier to hide when the police were actually looking for her. She'd been out of breath when she started running from all the false coughing, but now, eleven blocks later, she was positively panting for air, and this time she wasn't faking it.

With five blocks to go, Sabrina slowed to a steady jog, trying to control her racing heart and clearly audible attempts to regain her breath. Around her the night had started out chilly, but now she felt hot, sweat was in danger of dripping off her by the time she staggered, half dead, into the seemingly deserted park.

Now came the hard part. Ella hadn't said exactly where the others would be hiding. Sabrina allowed herself to slip into a brisk walk as she searched. They weren't in the picnic shelter or the kiddy pool. The park building was closed and both bathrooms were locked. The tennis courts were deserted as well. Sabrina had one last option, she set off for the playground, her tired feet skidding dully over the grass.

"Psst!" It was Dawn, pressing her eye to one of the windows in the tunnel, she beckoned to Sabrina, who wasted no time in joining her.

"Did it work?" Rita whispered as soon as Sabrina had climbed over her to sit in the tunnel. Sabrina didn't answer right away, she waited until after she'd hugged Tessa to within an inch of her life. When both twins were satisfied that their degree of wishing for the other had been conveyed, Sabrina returned to Rita's inquiry.

"It kind of worked," she admitted. "I got away, but someone else from the orphanage saw; they must've called the police. And, well…" Sabrina hesitated to tell them about Gabby. That was a subject she did not want to bring up when any loud noise, such as Dawn berating her, might lead to certain imprisonment. Unfortunately she was not given the choice.

"And what?" Dawn prompted. "Wait, tell once we're somewhere else, we can't stay in here if the police are going to be looking for us. It's too obvious. Come on."

The group squeezed out of the tunnel and made their way off the jungle gym as quickly as they could. Dawn avoided all the streetlights as she led the others to a grove of tall pines about ten yards away from the playground. The trees had obviously been there for a long time. Only three of them stood there, rustling in the slight breeze and providing a prime hiding place for five runaway girls. The trunks were wide and smooth, but a multitude of long branches formed an almost perfect ladder up to the top.

"Go as high as you can and stay there." Dawn ordered, and wasted to time in pulling herself up to the nearest branch and beginning her ascent. The others followed, a little more slowly than would have been preferable. Alyssa was not quite tall enough to cross some of the larger gaps on her own, Tessa had to stay behind to act as footstool. At last they reached the top, or at least the highest they could go without breaking the branches, and settled down to wait. Dawn propped herself against the trunk and extended her legs along a branch, letting herself relax for all of five seconds before she turned to Sabrina, sitting next to Tessa with her legs over one branch and her neck resting on another.

"OK, you were saying? What went wrong?"

Sabrina groaned. "Well, there was this little girl, my roommate and she kind of figured everything out, like, everything."

Dawn only just managed to contain herself before she shouted; as it was, her whisper felt like a blade in the darkness. "Where is she now? Is she in danger of telling someone?"

"She'd still at the orphanage, but not for long. You see, she kind of, well, she blackmailed me. She won't tell anyone, but…" Sabrina trailed off, trying to avoid Dawn's eye.

"But she's blackmailing you," the leader prompted, "What does she want?"

Sabrina cringed, but somehow forced out the truth. "She wants to join up with us. She made me promise."

Dawn had never come so close to swearing in her life. "Great, just what we need: another blackmailing newbie." Almost at once she regretted it, and said so, grateful that no one could see her shame in the shadows.

"I know this probably isn't the right thing to say," Sabrina started, "but she's really smart. She worked out our situation pretty much from a smell alone. That could be useful."

"A smell?" Dawn raised an eyebrow that no one could see.

"Yeah, apparently both me and Ella smell like an old barn."

Dawn almost swore again, and the effort not to left her speechless. Rita filled the silence. "Wow, she must have one insane nose."

"She has an insane everything," Sabrina grumbled, "and we're supposed to pick her up behind that weird old restaurant near her school tomorrow — otherwise she'll tell everyone."

Dawn was saved the bother of answering by the slamming of a car door from not too far away. Everyone froze, holding their breath, hoping with all their might that it wasn't the police.

They stayed there in the trees, frozen, for the next half hour, afraid to talk or even breathe too much. By the time they heard the car door slam again and the engine start up once more, every one of them was sore from holding their uncomfortable positions for so long. Alyssa was the first to speak.

"Was that the police?"

Dawn shrugged. "I don't know, but we better stay here just in case it wasn't."

"What time is it?" Rita wanted to know.

Tessa consulted her watch. "Just after midnight. We've got a while to wait for Ella. Do you think it's safe to sleep up here?"

"NO!" Several whispered voices joined in universal opposition.

"Kidding," Tessa giggled softly.

They were silent, each listening to her own thoughts as the hours passed. No more cars stopped at the park that night, and by the time the sun rose most of their worries had been appeased.

46

Ella was dead tired; even with the nap she'd taken the day before she could barely keep her eyes open. It was nearing two in the morning, with no word from the police. That was a good thing, but with every minute that passed, Ella grew more paranoid. All the night aides had returned to their posts looking worn out and she was now assigned to tidying the lounge. It was not a difficult job, but Ella did wonder if they'd merely told her to do this so they wouldn't have her in the way as they talked about her possible involvement in Sabrina's escape. But no, they didn't suspect her. At least she hoped they didn't.

Ella finished quickly, putting the few stray checkers back into their box and replacing one or two books on the small shelf in the corner. There really wasn't much for her to do, so she turned to her next objective: the files in Mr. Wallace's office. Ella climbed the stairs to the main entryway quickly and checked for any signs of life before scurrying into the open and over through Mr. Wallace's door.

The office too was deserted and Ella wasted no time in returning to the desk. Sabrina's papers were still there. A little guiltily she picked up the file and began to read. *Sabrina Mantz. Admitted to Redfield Social Services Center on 10/5/2009.*

Height: 5'6". Weight: 123 lbs. Date of birth: 1/28/1995. Former address: 1528 Cadley Ave, #209, Redfield; and 6847 Ridger drive, Blighton Valley. Reason for admission: Survivor of domestic abuse; run-away protection.

Ella skimmed over the medical information and the police report and stopped on the third sheet to look at the Statement From Parent/Guardian.

David Mantz: " 'How dare you ask about her, you backstabbing cop! Get out of here before I drive you out.' " Natalie Hemmons: "a violent and yet nonverbal response involving a curtain rod and a heavy dictionary. Now in custody for assault on a police officer."

There was nothing useful in the folder, so Ella started to put it back when the file underneath it caught her eye. It belonged to a girl named Gabriella Wandor — that wasn't alphabetical order. No, there had to be a different system, no one could be *that* disorganized. Ella searched Gabriella's folder for any sign of a connection. Her birthday was in June, so that didn't match, and she was two years younger than Sabrina, even though Sabrina had been put in the youngest dorm room... The other girls in there, they were...what? Leanne, Brooke and...Gabby! Gabriella! She was that weird girl with the red hair. Ella couldn't help herself; she dove into the folder with a guilty interest.

According to the file, Gabby had arrived at the orphanage a year before, after a psychopathic murderer named Kristin Allerman had killed her single mother. Allerman had since been caught and sentenced to death. Ella's eyes widened. Allerman was a very familiar name and she knew where she'd heard it before.

Shaken and confused, Ella carefully replaced the folders on Mr. Wallace's desk. She returned to the lounge and sat at the table, head in her hands. For now all she wanted was to go back to the barn, to talk everything over with Sabrina, and ask Dawn if she had ever heard about Kristin Allerman. After all, they shared a last name; maybe Dawn was related to a serial killer. Guiltily, Ella thought that would explain a lot.

The early birds were just rising when Ella finished her shift that morning. None of the aides looked particularly chipper. Tori seemed to have calmed down a bit, but now looked veritably depressed. Rick and Harold stared silently out the window waiting for the day aides to come; both of them looked especially grave.

There were only two day aides, a man and a woman. They were looking especially perky and bright, until Harold told them about Sabrina's escape. The woman sagged in her coat and the man sighed ominously.

"Absolutely awful. Have you heard back from the police?" The woman looked a little apprehensive.

"No," Tori admitted, "so you two will have to be on alert for that, too."

The man nodded understandingly. "Don't worry — we can handle it from here. You guys look like you could use some sleep."

Ella nodded fervently and opened the door of the orphanage. The van stood waiting for her. There was only one worry left in her mind as she drove to the park. A thousand things could have gone wrong between the time Sabrina ran and now.

The park was deserted. Ella saw no one as she parked and set off for the jungle gym. No one was there, either, but before Ella had time to get even more worried, she was being tackled to the ground. Rita grinned at her maliciously, but got off and let Ella stand up.

"Good morning! We were about to get worried," Rita told her.

"Yeah, so was I." Ella was a bit disgruntled by the overly strong greeting, but was glad to see her friend nonetheless. "Hey Rita, where are the others?"

Rita grinned again and pointed to the giant pine tree at the edge of the park. The rest of the Barn Brigade was standing just inside its lowest branches, and when Ella looked their way, Dawn waved at her.

Back in the van, after she'd been congratulated and praised by her friends, Ella turned to Dawn in curiosity, suddenly remembering about Kristen Allerman, the murderer. She worked toward the subject carefully.

"Hey Dawn, I want to ask you something."

Dawn looked skeptical, but curious. "OK... What?"

Ella took a deep breath; everyone in the car was listening by now. "So, last night I caught sight of Sabrina's files in Mr. Wallace's office — you know, that guy who was on the radio? He's the head of the Social Services Center. Anyway, I saw Sabrina's file and thought I'd make sure there was nothing incriminating in it. There wasn't, and it looks like your parents didn't tell the police anything either, Sabrina."

"Good," Tessa said. "Did they fight them?"

Ella cringed. "Yeah, your mom's in jail for assault of an officer. Did you know that Sabrina?"

"Yeah," Sabrina said, "they told me. It's not as if I care though. It just lowers the chance of me ever seeing her again."

No one really wanted to try and refute Sabrina's cold statement, so Ella went on.

"Well, when I was done with Sabrina's file, I saw that the one underneath belonged to Gabby. I thought it was a little weird that they were next to each other, since Gabby's last name is Wandor, so I looked in it and it said — "

"Wait." Dawn turned to her with a confused expression. "Who's Gabby?"

"Sabrina hasn't told you yet?"

Sabrina sighed in exasperation. "She's the girl I was talking about. The blackmailer."

"She blackmailed you?" Ella interrupted herself.

"Yes, she figured everything out and said she'd be my accomplice if I let her join us. When I told her no, she said she'd tell everyone about everything if I didn't let her. So yeah, she blackmailed me."

"That little...!" Ella was fuming. "She has no right to do that!"

"Yeah, I know," Dawn said, "but I've decided it's fine because she managed to figure everything out on her own, and that kind of brain could be very useful to us. Anyway — what were you saying about her file?"

Ella had almost forgotten about it. "Oh! On Gabby's intake form it said her mother was killed by a woman with Dawn's last name." Ella turned to face her friend as they crossed the railroad tracks. "Do you have an aunt or anything named Kristin?"

Dawn's eyes flew open wide and she stared at Ella in silent disbelief, her eyebrows arched in a line of dread. Her lips were slightly parted and between them Ella could just hear the slight hiss of her panicked breath.

"Kristin Allerman is your mother?" Ella had suspected as much, however grossly twisted the conclusion might be; it made sense that a woman who could burn her own children would be capable of murdering again.

Dawn nodded, licking her lips; she leaned back against her seat shivering slightly. The whole van was silent, each girl holding her breath, waiting for Dawn's reaction. It never came; instead, Ella spoke up once more.

"Dawn? That's not all. I thought you'd want to know. She was caught by the police and sentenced to death."

Dawn's eyes were cold, staring into space, the gray sky reflected in her irises. Ella could see where her bottom lip was caught between her teeth. She'd seen Dawn draw blood that way before. The leader's face twitched with tiny spasms of emotion that Ella couldn't name. Finally she gave voice to her rage.

"She deserves it." As much as Dawn meant it, there was something besides hate in the back of her heart, distant memories of a mother's touch, her sleepy smile, her voice, her laugh, her eyes. Dawn looked away as her eyes began to sting. Never once as a child had she thought the woman who fed her and clothed her would become a murderer. Even now she could hardly believe it. She didn't want to think of herself as a killer's daughter. She may be a thief, but robbery and murder were related only as closely as the word "crime" could pull them. They were as much alike as Dawn and her mother.

47

Later that day, the Barn Brigade, united and back in the Barn at last, sat down in council to discuss the issue of Gabby. Sabrina had already told her story in more depth and been heartily welcomed back. Now the girls were ready to turn to the more pressing matter.

"Let's go around and say our opinions one at a time," Sabrina suggested. "Tess, you can go first."

Tessa looked slightly self-conscious, but cleared her throat nonetheless. "I think the answer's clear. If Gabby's going to tell on us, we have to do what she says. Besides, if what Sabrina says is true, about her deductive skills, then we'll be gaining a valuable Brigadier, don't you think?"

Rita nodded and so did Alyssa, but the others weren't so sure.

Ella put in her two cents. "She has a lot of energy and bright red hair. Don't you think that would make her a bit conspicuous?" Ella turned to Dawn on her other side. "What do you think?"

"I don't think we have any choice but to take her in, but I don't want her nosing through everything and finding out all our secrets. It's unnerving, not to mention rude. Sabrina makes it sound like she's psychic and I feel safer living with a herd of kleptomaniacs," she swept an arm in front of her, indicating the group, "than I'd feel living with a mind-reader. She'd probably find out about my mom and the whole murder thing and I don't want to be cross-examined by a twelve year old. What do you think, Sabrina?"

Sabrina had to think for a minute. As much as she hated to admit it, she admired Gabby: her bottomless optimism, her friendly smile, and her overly active — though usually correct — imagination. She shrugged. "I agree, it's inevitable that she'll come to live with us. We'll have a ball making more accommodations though." There was a general glancing at Alyssa's slightly squished straw dog bed.

Dawn sighed. "I don't know how we'll all get along, and seven is a bit much for this barn, but we'll have to just make it work. There's no alternative." With that the debate was closed, for although Dawn had officially renounced her power, she still possessed the air of unquestionable authority, and the Barn Brigade valued and respected her decision.

The rest of the day was spent in almost pleasant preparation for Gabby's arrival. With all the chaos that had transpired during Sabrina's absence, the barn was in need of tidying. Ella read to them out of *Winnie the Pooh* while they worked and Dawn and Rita used another sheet and a cast off towel to make a dog bed for Gabby. It turned out to be extra lucky they'd gone to the Salvation Army, because most of what they'd selected for Alyssa would fit Gabby too. By two o'clock they were ready to go. Sabrina happened to know that Kazure Community School got out at three, so they had plenty of time to appear behind the restaurant near there.

48

Gabby was far too hyper for school that day. She found it difficult to even listen to her peers, let alone her teachers. In her backpack she had stashed her toothbrush and hairbrush, two books, two complete outfits, and a few other small possessions. By the time her teacher finally dismissed them, her leg hurt from bouncing and she had been told off for not paying attention no fewer than eleven times.

Gabby was supposed to go to Spanish club after school on Mondays, but instead waited just long enough so that her companions from the orphanage wouldn't see her sneaking off. The restaurant she'd decided to wait behind was only three blocks from her school. She set off running towards the restaurant, paying heed to avoid any glances from her classmates. It was hard to run in a backpack and even with the weather growing steadily chillier as October progressed, she found herself sweating under her sweater long before she reached the alley.

The restaurant itself was known for being a little bit eccentric. Rumor had it that before it was remodeled there had been cockroaches and rats there, and that some of them had stayed around even after the building had been cleaned up.

Most trash stinks. Gabby had become familiar with this fact early in the course of her twelve years, but the garbage behind this restaurant was beyond stinky. Luckily, Gabby didn't have to wait around. Though she'd never seen the van before, she recognized the girl driving it. Ella pulled up beside her and someone in the back seat opened the door for her. Gabby got into the van, crawling over someone to sit in the middle and all the while staring at the group of girls who sat in front of her.

The door was slammed, and as she buckled her seatbelt, Gabby scrutinized the group before her. She'd thought it would be only Ella, Sabrina and Tessa, but it turned all the Brigadiers had come. A grinning blonde girl Gabby had climbed over stuck her hand out and grabbed Gabby's, shaking it vigorously.

"I'm Rita. I can't wait for it to snow, do you like snow?"

Gabby instantly took to her, another girl with boundless energy and a flair for spontaneity, verging on randomness. She grinned back. "I like snow a lot. I didn't know there would be this many of you."

Identical heads popped up from the back seat.

"You're twins? You made it sound like Tessa was younger than you, and then I thought she'd be older because I saw her." Gabby jabbed her thumb at the front seat where Dawn raised her eyebrows sarcastically. "Come on, I don't really look that much like them, do I?"

Sabrina giggled and Tessa looked slightly miffed. "That's Dawn," she explained. "We're not related."

Gabby nodded. "OK, so that's Dawn and she's Rita..." Gabby pointed at Alyssa. "Who are you?"

Alyssa had been staring at Gabby with a mixture of amusement and disbelief. She quickly collected herself and smiled.

"I'm Alyssa. I'm pretty new to the barn too."

"Sweet! Thanks for taking me in, by the way, all of you." There was a strange silence during which Sabrina pulled a discreet and meaningful face-palm.

"You do know that you blackmailed us, right?" Dawn tried to emulate Ella when she said it, sounding not too harsh, but just disapproving enough to let Gabby know they meant business.

"Yeah — sorry about that." Gabby gazed out the window. She seemed completely unperturbed by the teetering situation around her.

Dawn shook her head. "Never mind. You're not the first."

Alyssa squirmed uncomfortably.

Tessa was quick to change the subject, directing the conversation out of the realm of treachery. "I know it's not exactly a cheery subject, but I suppose we'd better give you an idea of how we each ended up at the Barn, huh?"

"Yes!" Gabby's enthusiastic response caused raised eyebrows, even from those who'd lived with Rita for some months. "I'd like to know."

Alyssa went first, giving a brief outline of her story. Since Gabby had already heard about the twins, Rita went next. She didn't cry nearly so much this time and Ella's story went quickly as well so all too soon Dawn was on the hook once again.

"Do you mind if I go last? I'm not exactly good at talking about this yet. Do you feel comfortable going next, Gabby? How come you're living in the orphanage?"

"I'm not anymore."

"OK then, how come you were?" Dawn already knew, of course, but thought it best to pretend like she didn't, maybe just so she could get the full story. That was not what Gabby wanted to hear, however.

"You already know. Sabrina told you, didn't she?"

Even though she'd made it sound like a question, this was clearly not the case. Dawn frowned.

"You're right. I just want to hear it first hand, that's all."

"You're trying to avoid telling me about yourself, aren't you?"

Once again, this was not really a question; Dawn was beginning to see what Sabrina meant about this kid being a pint-sized Poirot. She decided to try and fake her out.

"You're right. I'm avoiding the subject. But I promise to tell you once you're done. You can tell I'm not lying, can't you?"

Gabby nodded even as she started to tell her story. "My mom never got married. I never knew my dad; they split up while she was pregnant. When I was eight, my mom was out at a café when a madwoman killed her with a baseball bat for *no reason*. The killer was arrested; she was sentenced to death for murdering nine people including her own husband and children."

Dawn choked and the others saw her visibly shiver in the front seat. Alyssa laid a tentative hand on her shoulder. Suddenly Dawn whipped her head around and looked back pleadingly at Gabby.

"Say that again?"

"She was sentenced to death for murdering nine people including her own husband and children."

"Her... her husband?"

"Yeah, she pushed him off a bridge."

Another shudder ran through Dawn's body and tears ran down her distressed face though she made no sound. This seemed to be one situation Gabby couldn't figure out; she stared at Dawn, completely still, calculating and concerned. Ella finally broke the tension. "Would you like me to explain, Dawn?"

Dawn's eyes widened and she shook her head as though hypnotized. "N-no, I can do it." She spoke so softly that only Ella heard her.

Courteously, Ella pulled the van to the side of the road and put it into park so Dawn could talk. They were settled on a county road with little traffic, about three quarters of the way to the Barn. Dawn unbuckled her seat belt and turned around, hoisting herself to sit on the container between the seats. She looked at the floor and took a deep breath. The shock of discovering her father's murder had reawakened the pain she felt in the telling, and it was difficult for her to speak, but bravely, she swallowed, and began.

49

It had been a long night. Dawn had once again told her story. Finally knowing the truth about her father's death was upsetting and disorienting. How long had her family lived in ignorance of her mother's madness? How many people had she killed while they were still living together?

Almost as soon as they had reached the barn, Ella had had to bid them farewell and drive into Redfield again, for her second shift at the orphanage. The others were left to complete their routine in silence, feeling the echo of Dawn's story. Gabby didn't like to show it, but her mind and emotions had been utterly jumbled up in the conversation by the side of the road. She no longer knew what to think of Dawn. She knew it wasn't right to fear her just because her mother was a monster, but somehow Gabby found herself utterly cowed by the leader.

It was not the overwhelming obedience and respect that Alyssa had experienced. Dawn had changed since then — not a lot, but enough to make a difference in her demeanor. Gabby shivered as she washed the dinner dishes, remembering Dawn's reaction. She hadn't screamed or wailed, but somehow her dripping eyes and devastated face gave off such a stream of tangled emotions, such an intense force of feeling, Gabby felt she could almost taste it. Not sure where to go from there, Gabby tried looking at Dawn as a complete person, not past and present, as if the once-desolate twelve-year-old still existed within her strong, tall body. And perhaps she did. Dawn would carry those memories for the rest of her life.

Gabby sighed. She felt a little sad at the thought, but at least she knew that although Kristen Allerman had killed Gabby's mother, her own husband, and her son, she had murdered only *eight* people. The ninth was still alive, and fighting for her existence with all her skills. Gabby decided she was glad Dawn had survived. *Even if I don't know it yet, she's probably a beautiful person. I don't have to worry about her. She'll do just fine.*

The next morning, Ella returned, looking half dead from yet another sleepless night spent pretending to agonize over missing children. She pulled into the barn and staggered down the ladder.

"Mail for you." Ella tossed something to Rita. "I was assigned to sort the incoming mail and found that. It's addressed to you, so I thought it wouldn't hurt to bring it here. I'm really curious. What does it say?" Ella looked over Rita's shoulder curiously and was quickly joined by the rest of the Barn Brigade, but all Rita was aware of was the letter.

It was in an ordinary envelope, the kind with the peel-off back. On the front was written her name, Rita Avis. Beneath that was the address of the Social Services Center. Somehow it felt strange to be being contacted through a place where she did not live. There was no return address, but all the same, Rita recognized the handwriting. With shaking fingers she tore open the envelope. She read the letter aloud in the quiet of the basement, everyone tense with hope.

> *Dear Rita,*
> *We're so sorry it has been so long. We spent six months trying to obtain a suitable visa for Namono. It took so long*

because we could not be seen together, or by either of our families. We never actually got the visa because we were spotted by one of my uncles and chased out by the police. You are lucky to have such kind and fair police in America. These people should not call themselves vessels of the law. They are unfair, uneducated, prejudiced and violent. At least the ones who followed us. They kept shouting insults. I'm glad you weren't there to hear them. It was awful. As much as we know we aren't any of the awful things they called us, it still hurt.

We escaped into Rwanda and are currently staying here until we can get enough resources to return to the US. We're sorry, but we don't know how long that might take — anywhere from a few months to a year or more. Don't worry about it though. You're in good hands and we'll be back to reunite with you as soon as we can. We love you. Please don't give up hope. We're sorry for having to leave as we did. We hope to make it up to you when we return.

Love,
Masa and Namo

Rita's eyes filled with tears as Tessa wrapped her arms around her from behind. Alyssa squeezed her hand and Sabrina patted her arm. Gabby, and the others too far away to touch her, showed their support with an almost palpable warmth.

"They're alive! They're alive," Rita laughed happily. "I can't believe it, oh my gosh, I can't believe it!" Tears rolled down her smiling cheeks and she hugged the letter to her chest, pulling its words into her heart. She loved her mothers intensely, and right now she felt at home with the girls around her, another sort of family. She smiled again, taking in her circumstances.

These were all girls forsaken by fate, battered and beaten by the ways of luck and fortune. Yet they had pulled through to face each other now, united in the bond that comes with overcoming sadness. For right now at least, the barn was their home and they were each other's sisters.

ABOUT THE AUTHOR

Nora Tisel Farley began writing in fourth grade. She has since taken many classes at the Loft Literary Center in her home town of Minneapolis, and studied creative writing at the Minnesota Institute for Talented Youth (MITY). At MITY she completed her first short story, *How Not to be a Lion Tamer*, and discovered a love for rhyming poetry. *The Barn Brigade* began as a short story as well, but evolved so quickly that Nora put it to the test as her very first National Novel Writing Month (NaNoWriMo) novel instead. Nora, 15, is eager to write another book next November, with her brother and writing partner, Owen Farley, author of *The True History*, to encourage her.

Made in the USA
Lexington, KY
04 August 2012